LUCKY DAY EVERY DAY

LUCKY DAY

★ ★ ★ ★ ★

EVERY DAY

A Novella by Sean Hansen

INKWATER
PRESS

PORTLAND • OREGON
INKWATERPRESS.COM

*Scan this QR Code
to learn more about
this title*

Publisher: Inkwater Press | www.inkwaterpress.com

Paperback
ISBN-13 978-1-62901-318-3 | ISBN-10 1-62901-318-8

Kindle
ISBN-13 978-1-62901-319-0 | ISBN-10 1-62901-319-6

Printed in the U.S.A.

1 3 5 7 9 10 8 6 4 2

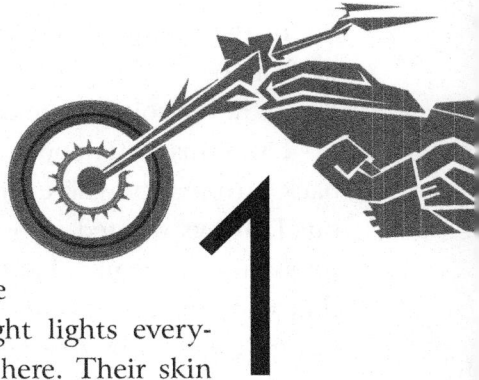

I t was a typical day for me, Hossan, just like any other in Alpha city, the richest and most powerful city in the world. Everything was clean here, bright lights everywhere, and everyone was happy to be here. Their skin was pure white, their eyes as bright blue as the sky over Alpha, and they always had wide smiles on their faces, twenty-four seven, no matter what. Though the fact that the Perfects always smiled may be discouraging, these people were looked up to like super heroes. No, that's an understatement. They appeared as gods to me and all of the other regular humans. I worked as a janitor in one of the thousands of shopping malls in Alpha city, mopping floors and cleaning windows from seven in the morning until eight at night. I felt so small and insignificant compared to them, but I also felt lucky to be able to stand so close to them. As each second passed, it seemed that there were at least a thousand new Perfects walking around me. I looked up at them, but they wouldn't bother to even glance at me.

I continued mopping, and suddenly I heard a voice calling out to me.

"You are amazing!" I turned and saw that it was a billboard ad for stylish new clothes.

"I can see it in your eyes!" The person talking from the billboard was none other than one of the Perfects: a beautiful, elegant bikini-clad Perfect woman. Even though the words came from an ad, it felt great hearing one of them say those kinds of things to me. I closed my eyes and, for a second, I imagined myself as one of them – tall, strong, rich, and beautiful.

"Do you dare to reach up to the stars and challenge the world?" The advertisement finished.

In the middle of my daydreaming, one of my coworkers came up from behind me and said in a degrading tone, "Get over it, man. You're never going to be one of them. No way!"

I was instantaneously shot out of my blissful daydream and back into reality where I belonged. I tried not to let it bother me, but I always wanted to be like one of the Perfects, no matter how impossible it seemed. I hated being a human. Being a human meant that you were lesser than dirt and that you'd never amount to anything. It was a miserable existence for all of us.

My shift ended and I headed to the employee locker room. It was late, half past eight and I was extremely tired. I unzipped my janitor uniform. It was all white to mimic the cleanliness and perfection of the Perfects and Alpha city. I placed my uniform in my locker and took my casual clothes. Blue jeans, a black shirt and a brown jacket.

"See you tomorrow," muttered Bartek, a co-worker and long-time friend.

As soon as I changed, I walked through the halls to grab my pay on the way out. I approached a counter with a glass barrier that stood between me and Lidiya. As soon as she saw my face, she sighed loudly to express her disgust. Lidiya always thought very highly of herself for some reason even though she was just a regular human like me and all of the other workers who got their pay from her.

Lidiya passed my pay through a space at the bottom of the glass. It consisted of a bunch of coins and only a few bills. It was enough to live at least. I exited the building with the money in my coat pocket. When I walked outside, I looked up at the shopping mall where I worked to admire the architecture. If I had to guess, it had to be at least fifty stories tall. But it was nothing compared to the other buildings in Alpha.

Alpha was like a safe haven. In Alpha city there's little to no crime or poverty either. Alpha was clean and well maintained every day and to top it all off, the only cares that the Perfects had were to party, keep up with trends, follow celebrity news, and enjoy being young. It would have been a dream come true for me to live here as one of the Perfects. Who wouldn't want to live here?

I always loved commuting through Alpha city. Before and after work I would always try to explore Alpha as much as I could because it was so interesting to me. I'd love to live in this city but I can't as dictated by law, and the little money I have. Beautiful, exciting, and safe. Those were probably the best words that I could use to describe Alpha City.

As I walked down the sidewalk I noticed two Perfects out of the thousands of other Perfects walking around me in the crowd. They both wore the same black uniforms with gold trimmings on the edges, along the arms and down to the legs. My eyes fixed on them as they walked past me. They were security agents to Mayor Rollins. I always wondered what it would be like to be an agent. I'm sure it must have been tedious in many ways, but it would still be better than where I was in life.

But what stood out most about them were the large handguns in their holsters that were very clearly visible. Alpha city passed a law that prevented guns to be in the possession of any humans, but it didn't help. Guns were so common in Roderic, where the humans lived, that if you funneled through any ordinary dumpster, you would most likely find at least one.

As I kept walking, I passed a large, brightly lit building. It had a sign in bright lights that said *Formula H*. The "H" in Formula H stands for health. Every day, millions of Perfects visited the Formula H building. Only Perfects were allowed to use the Formula H building, where they would relax on a long, soft bed built just for them and they'd be pumped with Formula H till they were full. Formula H to them was like clean water to us. It made their skin appear white and their bodies stay young. I had no idea what was in Formula H; humans weren't allowed to use the stuff. Just as humans weren't allowed to use Formula H, we also weren't allowed to see a Perfect's real face. Nobody had ever seen one because a Perfect wouldn't bother to lift a finger for us let alone permit us to see their bare face. Nobody would ever force them to take their masks off either; we wouldn't want to hurt their beautiful faces.

The only differences between the Perfects were their hairstyles and clothes, although all of them followed the trends and therefore wore many of the same sort of clothes and hairstyles. Most of their personalities weren't too different from each other, though I didn't care at all, nor did anyone else. It made no difference; their beauty, fame, and sense of taste made them all incredible. The only real difference between the Perfects was located on the forehead of their masks, where barcodes were imprinted for identification.

I walked up to a subway platform that I always used after work to get home to Roderic. With a poverty rate of over 43.3 percent, Roderic city was apparently created to be poor. There wasn't ever a single one of the Perfects on the subway to Roderic. Why would they ever bother coming down to Roderic anyway? Pretty much anyone in Roderic who wasn't making money, illegally that is, worked in Alpha city. Of course there were jobs in Roderic, but they didn't pay nearly as well as jobs in Alpha, though the pay wasn't all that grand to begin with. What the Perfects told us is that we were lucky to be working for them. The harder we worked, the better humans we would become.

I was one of those people. I always rejected doing crime in order to make more money. I never thought it was the right thing to do. But doing crime to make money usually resulted in a higher pay than what I got paid. So seeing a person getting mugged in a dark alleyway was a pretty common sight. If I robbed enough people who weren't paying enough attention to their stuff, I might have been able to make more than I normally did. It was tempting. Sometimes I thought I could do it if I were fast enough and didn't think about it too much. But I couldn't allow myself to do something like that. I couldn't let myself become a member of the walking dead, like the rest of the humans in Roderic.

Most people got used to seeing others being beaten or getting high on the streets or in the alleyways. But no one, including myself, ever got used to constantly looking over your shoulder, fearing that today could be the day where you ended up as another battered and broken body on the streets of Roderic... but not without first having your wallet taken.

I sat down on the cold, hard plastic benches in the train. It was packed with dozens of people. They were all humans, of course. The train then accelerated away from the platform and the city got further and further away. Since it was an elevated train, I was able to see all of the people walking on the sidewalk. There were subways that work just as well, but I always preferred using the elevated train where I could see the lights of Alpha city as I returned home.

In the middle of my journey, the tracks that were within the border of Alpha were well maintained. The train was practically silent as it rode along Alpha's tracks. However, I soon heard a loud a loud clang from where I sat in the train. It came from the tracks, and it was followed by more violent-sounding clangs that rattled the whole train. I didn't have to look outside to know that the tracks here were barely holding together. There were pieces of the guard rails along the tracks that had fallen into the streets and sidewalks. This was how I knew that I was back in Roderic, where I belonged.

I looked down through the window to see the train pass over the Big Gate. The Big Gate was pretty self-explanatory. It was a giant metal arched structure with big, bright neon lights on top that spelled out, "Welcome to Alpha City!" It was the largest, most popular way to get in and out of Alpha. Thousands of humans walked through it every minute. There were usually Perfect guards posted around the Big Gate with big guns in order to ensure safety and security. Safety and security was always a luxury that was completely out of reach of us humans.

I arrived at my stop and headed down to the sidewalk, where thousands of other humans roamed around aimlessly. As I walked along the sidewalk, I passed familiar faces I'd seen over and over again. I passed Hendri, the owner of a small motorcycle shop. Most of the motorcycles he sold were just motorized bicycles and dirt bikes. He stole normal bikes by cutting off the chains that were used to tie them down, then he brought the bikes to his shop where he installed motors onto them. Since he was one of the only humans who knew how to do this, his shop was popular.

I peered through the window of Hendri's motorcycle shop and saw the love of my life. A bright red, beautiful brand new motorcycle. It had a four-stroke, liquid-cooled engine with a digital fuel injector, putting out 649cc, all packed into a high tensile steel frame. With the purr of the engine and its handles in my hands, my life would feel complete. Of course, I could never afford something like that.

There was also Jodoc. He worked and managed a small stand on the sidewalk, selling magazines, gum and small snacks. Sometimes he'd break in and rob other stores of not just their money, but their snacks, magazines and gum as well. He did this so that he could acquire more inventory without having to spend money for it. At the same time, this eliminated any competition. He kept a gun behind his counter, in case anyone tried to steal from him. One time when a guy was complaining about how the snacks he sold sucked, I heard Jodoc yell at him, "If you don't like what I got then just drop it and walk away!" Then I heard him cock his gun, making that terrifying click sound that all guns made.

I would usually buy small snacks from him and pass it off as breakfast, lunch, and dinner. I'd never had a healthy meal; I didn't really have the time to cook for myself, nor the money. As I passed by each familiar face, I waved to them and they waved back.

I walked over to a line of people waiting to use a vending machine. The line stretched to the end of a block, and then around the corner as well. This vending machine didn't sell drinks or snacks, it sold lottery tickets. The lottery was not for cash prizes, though. It would allow the winner to actually become a Perfect and live in Alpha.

A long time ago, it was promised by the Mayor of Alpha city, Michael Rollins, that whoever won the lottery would be able to permanently live in Alpha city. They would be transformed into one of the Perfects, and live in luxury for the rest of their lives. I had dreamed of the day when that would happen to me, ever since it was first announced on TV. The day after the announcement, one of the vending machines was dropped off by a couple of the Perfects. That was the first time I'd ever seen one of them in person but also the last time I'd ever seen any of the Perfects in Roderic.

I remember that as soon as another machine was offloaded from the truck and turned on, people lined up, waiting for days to buy tickets. Everyone on the line quickly became impatient and angry. Scuffles would break out between the tired and hungry people. Often people would be randomly mugged while they waited on line. The muggers knew that the people waiting on line wouldn't let go of their place in line to stop the attack. Of course, there were many of the lottery ticket machines in Roderic, at least a million in the entire city. Even then, the lines still snaked around buildings and down blocks.

This all started about seventeen years ago. Because of the muggings and long waits, less and less people decided to buy the lottery tickets. A lot of people will tell you that they were afraid of being attacked. But you know what I think? I think most people just gave up on their dreams. I intended to stay faithful to my hopes and never give up on my dreams. I will become one of the Perfects, I thought.

It was finally my turn to buy a ticket. I stepped up to the tall metallic rectangle that was the lottery ticket machine. I pushed some of the coins from my pay into the machine's coin slot. I then pressed a button near the coin slot to get my ticket and out came a slip of paper from a different slot. The numbers were 7, 3, 19, 5, and 22. I shoved the slip of paper into my jacket pocket and walked off.

I couldn't think of a single person who wouldn't want to become a Perfect and live in Alpha city. There was a law saying that no human was allowed to live in Alpha city, which at the same time meant that no human was allowed to live in Alpha city. We were allowed to commute and work in Alpha city, but never to live there. Unless of course they were to be transformed into one of the Perfects by winning the lottery. This law didn't really matter, though. It's not like any human could ever afford to live anywhere in Alpha city for even a day.

Before I finally got to my apartment, I passed a bum who was sitting under a light pole. As I pulled out my keys from my pocket to unlock the front door, I took a quick glance at him. He was staring directly into the night sky with dead, empty eyes. He sat in an awkward position with his hands beside him. His arms shook wildly and they were covered in tiny, bloody holes. Beside him was a metal spoon, a lighter, a Zip-loc bag that was stained with blackish-brown gunk on the inside and a syringe, also stained with the same blackish-brown gunk.

I unlocked the main door and walked up the stairs to my room on the second floor. Just like the main door, the stairs were old and creaked as soon as I touched them. Most of the apartments in Roderic were falling apart like this one.

I unlocked the door and stepped into my tiny one-room apartment with a small window on the wall opposite the door. To my left upon entering was my bed. The sheets and the blanket were old and torn. To my right was a furnace I used for warmth during the winter. I always used my losing lottery tickets as kindling for the furnace. Most apartments in Roderic didn't have air conditioning or heating. Next to the furnace was a small TV that sat on top of a small counter. With the TV, I could hear about the winning lottery numbers and also watch shows, all broadcast from Alpha. They mostly featured celebrity news, new trends, and music videos.

I pulled off my jacket and threw off my shoes. I pulled out the ticket I bought today and set it on the counter. I walked over the floor, covered with hundreds more losing tickets. All of those losing lottery tickets were destined only to be burned in my furnace. I pulled back the covers and laid down on my bed. I looked at the clock on the wall. It was 12:00 am. It was time.

Suddenly a loud siren screamed across the city of Roderic. The booming sound of the alarm bounced off every building and flooded every alleyway. Then block by block, all of the lights were shut off and the streets were eventually cleared of all people. Even the bum who was sitting under the light pole was gone. The lights from Alpha city still shined on brightly without any sign of being turned off.

I wanted something to change in my life, something that would make things more exciting. It didn't have to be to live in Alpha city as one of the Perfects. But just something. Anything. Poverty, Filth, and Crime. Those were the words I could probably use to best describe Roderic. And with that thought, I fell asleep.

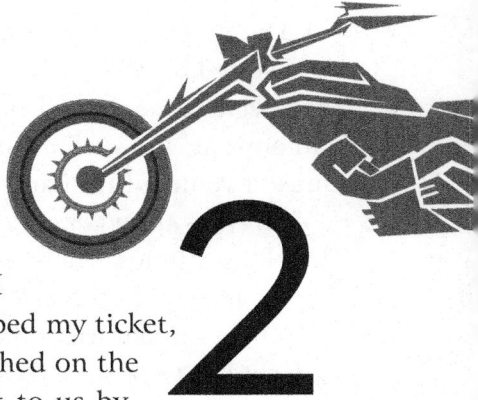

woke up the next morning in a haze. I threw off the covers and placed my bare feet on the cold wooden floor. I walked over to the countertop and grabbed my ticket, and made myself a cup of coffee. I switched on the TV and flipped to the channel brought to us by the Perfects. It featured a host who was well built, handsome and tall, just like most of the other Perfects. His voice was naturally loud and confident.

"Coming at you live from Alpha city! Right now, we're going to announce the numbers of the Lucky Day lottery! And later, we've got more hit music videos just for you!" The host then pointed over to a bikini-clad Perfect girl.

"Now check out sexy Stacy as she brings out the winning numbers!" he said as the camera panned and focused on the bikini girl.

She announced the numbers as they came onto the screen. Her voice was as beautiful as she was. "91, 53, 2, 23, and last but not least, 76."

I read the numbers on my ticket as she read them and quickly realized that I'd lost. The host then walked into shot and wrapped his left arm around her hip and pointed right at the camera.

"If those are the numbers on your ticket, well it's sure as hell your lucky day! Please submit the ticket as soon as possible. And if you didn't win this time, well don't you worry, friend! Because there is always another chance! So get all of the negativity and all that negative energy out of your system. Now get out there and buy those tickets!" he said loudly and proudly.

The camera then zoomed in on them to only show the two above their waist before they finished.

"And remember! Every day is a lucky day when you win…" The camera quickly zoomed in for a close up. "The Lucky Day lottery!"

The program switched over to commercials right afterwards.

I stared blankly at the screen as the realization of losing the lottery began to sink in. I had already figured that I wasn't going to win anyway. It's such a slim chance and I've already tried so many times. I've heard the same crap over and over again.

"There is always another chance."

I honestly lost track of how many times I'd heard that phrase. My feelings of disgust for living in Roderic and the hateful remorse of being a human was what fueled me to go on. I sometimes dwell, why couldn't I be born a Perfect? I stopped caring about things like how to take care of myself. I just want to leave my life of misery as a human and live the good life as a Perfect.

Every day was the same: I'd wake up and work. I took the usual elevated train to work, same as always. Before I got onto the train, I used one of the lottery ticket machines. It sat on the train station platform, lit brightly to make it extremely obvious. I liked this one because I could use this just before I got on the train at Roderic. I liked the convenience. When I got my lottery ticket, I looked down at my numbers, 2, 53, 9, 1, and 65. I then slipped the lottery ticket into my wallet. I felt hopeful that this would be the one that would make me a winner. My hope drained when my brain reminded me about how many times I'd lost.

When I got inside one of the train cars, a few people were sitting around. They all had their eyes to the ground with blank expressions on their faces. I took my seat, which was as far from any other person as possible. Out of nowhere, a man in a blue jacket quickly shuffled over and sat in the seat beside me. He could've chosen any of the other seats on the train, but he sat next to me. The man then reached into his jacket pocket and pulled out a large knife.

The man then poked me at my belly with the knife and yelled, "Gimme all your money!"

I raised up both of my hands in a show of surrender. I didn't have a weapon, and I had no idea how to fight. There was no way that I could get out of this situation.

"Okay, okay. Let's just take it down a notch. Alright?" I said trying to calm the man down.

I saw his face. His eyes only had the color of blood red and he had a long scar that stretched down his right cheek. The train was getting close to the next stop.

"C'mon! Let's fuckin' go already!" the man yelled angrily as he began to press the knife harder into my belly.

I looked past the man to see the other passengers. Most of them were large, tough-looking men, but every one of them was as quiet as a mouse. I slowly reached into my pocket and pulled out my wallet. The man quickly grabbed the wallet from my hand. He then stood up from the chair and pointed the knife into my face.

"If you follow me, you're dead! Got it!?" he yelled as the train stopped.

The man bolted out of the train as soon as it stopped. He slipped through the crowd of people as they began to walk onto the train. He disappeared into the crowd, and the doors of the train closed. The train's wheels started to move, and the train station where the man got off was getting further and further away. I felt angry, humiliated. My blood was boiling. I reached into my pocket and found only a few coins and an old, wadded-up paper bill.

On my way back to my apartment after work, I was still feeling angry. I decided to spend whatever money I had left on a couple of beers. I think getting a little drunk will take my mind off things. When I got into my apartment, I threw some of the losing lottery tickets into the furnace and sat on the side of my bed. I opened a can of beer and set the other one to my side as I grabbed the remote and turned on the TV. A music video was being broadcast from Alpha city. It showed a bunch of Perfect guys dancing around a Perfect girl in the center as she danced in front of a sports car. They danced to a booming song that was hugely popular right now.

She was Gisele Williams, a normal human turned into a Perfect megastar. The music video then switched to a shot of Gisele sitting between two guys. The guys slid their hands up and down her legs and breasts. It looked like she was enjoying the groping a lot. The music video soon ended and turned to a commercial.

The Perfect announcer spoke loudly with confidence, "Watch Gisele's incredible rise to fame in her new movie all about her. *I Wanna Be Perfect!* Watch it! It's the best shit!"

I feel so jealous of her, but I loved her. I'd watch her all day if I could.

Suddenly, I heard yelling coming from outside. The nagging of an old woman.

"What do you think you are doing, idiot!? Who do you think you are!? Don't you ignore me!"

That old lady just kept blabbing away so loudly at some poor soul. I had forgotten to close the window, but I didn't want to get up so I just tried to ignore it all. I was getting more and more annoyed as the yelling continued.

"Get lost, you junkie slut!" I heard.

It became increasingly harder to pay attention to the TV with all of the yelling. I slammed down my beer in frustration and stood up from my chair. I stormed over to my window and poked my head out.

"Shut up!" I yelled out.

I saw that it was Lidiya who was yelling from her apartment on the other side of the street. The second she saw my face from her window, she screamed at me.

"What the hell do you want!? What!? You're going to defend that bitch!? You know what you are!? A mangy dog! That's right! You're nothing but a fucking bitch!" She screamed and snarled at the top of her lungs.

Her voice rang through my head and continued to fuel my frustrations. I tried to ignore it but she was so loud and her obnoxiously raspy voice hardly made it bearable to hear her talk for even a second. It was bad enough that we work in the same place, but she also lived across the street from me.

I looked down and saw who Lidiya was yelling at. It was a woman. She stood under a lamppost, smoking a cigarette. I could see from my window that she looked like she was close to my age. She was wearing dark clothes, and she had pearl white skin, bright blue eyes, and short black hair. She smiled at my face from the other side of the street. I felt happy, and a little warm inside. I heard Lidiya was still yelling things at me from her apartment but I didn't care. I was too mesmerized seeing this unknown beauty's smile.

The unknown beauty then looked down at her watch, and quickly walked away into the darkness of the city. I looked up to see that Lidiya had left as well. I walked away from the window and slumped back into my chair. Once again sipping my beer, I wondered about that woman. I had no idea who she was, but I felt like I had fallen in love. Maybe.

I saw that the TV was still on. It was showing a music video, a different one from the one before, but I think they're all the same. I looked up to the clock, and saw that it had just turned 12:00 am. Before I knew it, the sound of the siren signaling the curfew roared through the city and through the walls of my apartment. Like clock-work, block by block, the city lights began to disappear. The TV and all of the lights in my apartment had turned off on their own. I sipped the last of my beer and went straight to sleep. I drifted off to my sleep while thinking about the woman on the street.

A few days later, it was my day off so I decided to roam around Roderic. As I walked down the sidewalk, I saw that everyone was reading the same newspaper. When I saw the front cover of the newspaper I realized why everyone was so interested in reading today's paper. The front cover showed the headline. *New Winner of the Lucky Day Lottery!* I had to do a double-take to be sure about what I was seeing. I quickly headed over to Jodoc's stand to pick up today's paper.

I couldn't believe what I was seeing. It read, *Citizen of Roderic city, Jurica Balgoy, is the newest winner of the Lucky Day lottery.* Jurica's face was printed all over the front cover with the headline. Suddenly, I felt like I've seen this guy before. With that thought, I immediately noticed a long scar stretching across Jurica's right cheek. No doubt, it was the guy who mugged me on the train the other day. He must've used my ticket to win. I could've sat in a different train car or something, and now my chances of winning were gone. That bastard was living the good life and I was still stuck here. I could feel my blood boil. Anger and regret began to build inside me.

"Dammit," I mumbled to myself, wanting to scream out like a madman.

I began to wander around with the newspaper in my hands. I skimmed from article to article trying to find something to take my mind off losing. Then I found something interesting. It was an article about previous winners of the Lucky Day lottery. It told about how none of the previous winners ever called or even attempted to contact their family or friends. It was like they just disappeared.

Whenever the Perfect version of the winners were asked about their family, they always replied with something like, "What family?"

I turned from page to page trying to find something else in the newspaper. An article about a recent string of abductions in Roderic caught my eye. I read about how the people who were abducted were taken in the middle of the night with nobody to see it happen.

One of the victim's family was interviewed about their father being abducted. They said that he went out to get food from a market place, but he never returned. After ten minutes passed after the siren for the curfew went off, it was apparent to them that he wasn't coming back. They also mentioned that the market place that he said he was going to wasn't very far away at all.

Next to the article was a picture of the guy who was abducted. I was surprised that this guy got abducted because he had to have a couple hundred pounds over me and he had to be at least six feet tall. I couldn't imagine how someone like him could be abducted. The article continued to say that huge guys like him appeared to be the prime target in a long string of abductions all over Roderic. It said that authorities thought that the men were abducted so that people could make money by selling their organs. Once I read that part, I started to feel sick and threw away the newspaper. I then got over it all when I took a look at myself. I was not very tall or strong. Actually, at about five feet, five inches, I guessed I wouldn't be so much of a target to the abductors, which gave me some peace of mind, but it was still unnerving that abductions were now common in Roderic, especially when the people being abducted were huge, grown men.

I was walking on the sidewalk when suddenly I heard a familiar voice. "Hey Hossan!" I turned around to see my friend Erhan waving his arms around and screaming like an idiot.

"Hey! What's up!?" I turned and waved back to him.

Erhan invited me into his apartment.

"Come in! Come in! Sit anywhere!" he said.

I fumbled my feet through trash, old computer parts and tons of empty boxes. He sat down on one of the boxes and I did the same, setting one underneath myself. Erhan and I have known each other for a long time but the last time I talked to him was years ago. He pulled a carton of cigarettes out of one of the boxes and offered one to me. I politely declined.

Erhan casually stuck of the cigarettes in his mouth and started smoking. I took a closer look at the boxes and saw that they all had *www.ACGeneral.com* labeled on them.

"What is that?" I asked pointing to the URL printed on the boxes.

"It's the URL of the Alpha City General website. They sell pretty much everything there." He let out a little laugh, "I wouldn't be surprised if they started selling grenades. I usually get all my stuff from there," he explained.

"What kind of stuff?" I asked.

"Food, drinks, clothing, electronics. I get everything from that website," Erhan explained.

"How can you afford it all? Last time I remember, you told me that you didn't have a job. You were totally broke," I pointed out.

"Yeah, and I still don't. But the thing is, I actually don't really buy any of this stuff," he said as he stood up from his box chair.

Erhan walked over to a desk with a laptop and desktop wired together. He powered it on and up came small windows with lines and lines of random numbers and letters.

"What is this?" I asked, still confused.

"Let me ask you, what's your favorite drink?" Erhan asked as he pulled up the www.ACGeneral.com website.

"Um, beer, I guess," I replied.

"Okay then..." Erhan said as he tapped his fingers on the keyboard.

The computer displayed more lines of numbers and letters. New lines kept popping up and filling the screen every second. It seems so complicated yet Erhan is working as methodically as a surgeon.

"What is that?" I asked.

"It's COBOL. It's the type of code that ACGeneral uses on its website. I don't like using this code because it's so old but they use it so I gotta use it to hack into their website. What I do is I get into the website and place an order with fake, virtual money so that it looks like I'm paying, but really I'm not. I try to keep my purchases to a minimum so that I don't arouse suspicion," He explained, turning to me. "It's real easy, I can show you how to get like ten cases of beer." I shook my head in response.

"'No thanks, I'm good. I wouldn't understand it. Is it anything like our language?" I asked.

"I mean, if I mispronounce a word, you'd be able to understand what I meant, but if you write something wrong in programming it wouldn't work out at all," Erhan explained.

"So what? You just hoard all of this stuff for yourself?" I asked.

"No. Actually, I give most of it away."

"Who do you give it away to? Charity?"

"Well, the thing is, a lot of the people that live in this apartment don't have enough money to pay for food and other stuff once they've paid their rent. So, they come to me to get their extra stuff for them. And in return, they all pool in the rest of the money they have after paying their rent to pay my rent. If it wasn't for me, most of the people that live here would've probably starved to death. Everyone here loves me, and I love them, but this my baby," Erhan said pointing to his computer. "This website's security is complete shit if you ask me. But I'm glad that it's such shit, you know? It's saved plenty of people's lives."

Erhan shoved his burned out cigarette into an ashtray and he pulled out another one from a nearby box. He lit the new one and immediately went back to the computer.

"Just let me know, Hossan, if you want anything, anything at all and I'll get it to you. Free of charge," he said as he used one hand to hold his cigarette, blowing out the smoke, and he used his other hand to keep typing on the keyboard.

"No thanks. I'm not really into illegal stuff," I said.

"Alright, suit yourself," he replied.

Once I left Erhan's apartment, I realized that it was nighttime. I still felt a little bit frustrated about Jurica winning the lottery. Seeking a drain for my stress, I decided to go to the Roderic city park. It might be hard to believe that along with the disgusting garbage filled streets of Roderic there's a park. It wasn't that great of a park. I'm sure there were better ones in Alpha city. There were only patches of grass here and many of the trees are dead but I think it's an okay park.

There was one enormous hill where from the top you could clearly see Alpha city. There were other tall hills, but this one was the tallest. I decided to go up there again and have another look at Alpha City. I trudged to the summit. I used to climb this hill all the time as a little kid. When I got to the top, the view hadn't changed at all. I could see everything from the highways to the tallest skyscrapers. The sun had set and I could see every light in Alpha city. Every headlight and shining billboard was in my view from the top of this hill. The view was spectacular and almost therapeutic. I came up here any time I ever got angry or upset. The first time I saw Alpha city from this view was when I was just seven years old. I still remember how much in awe I was at that moment. But it doesn't matter now, that was over twenty years ago.

I got back to my apartment around ten at night, unlocked the main door and began walking upstairs to my room. When I tried to unlock the door, I dropped my keys. I sighed and bent down to pick them up. When I did, I heard a loud crash come from the main door. I looked over the railing of the stairs and saw someone was trying to break in. A large man I'd never seen before walked in. I became paralyzed in fear. I already had enough trouble with being mugged and didn't want anything else to happen to me. I frantically started picking at the keys. I quickly tried each key to unlock the door. His footsteps sounded closer and closer. I was so afraid that I had stopped thinking. I forgot which key was the right one.

I finally found the right key and stormed into my room as fast as I could. I quickly closed the door. I stood against the door, out of breath from my own fear. Multiple scenes began to play in my mind of a man in a coat attacking me. I finally caught my breath and calmed down. About twenty seconds had passed, and I was feeling pretty sure that the man in the coat wasn't after me. I was curious so I opened the door to see where the man had gone. I opened the door only an inch so that I could look without getting caught. I saw that the man was standing at the door across the hallway.

The man knocked on my neighbor's door. From where I was, I could see the intense anger on his face. At first, there was no answer at the door. Then the man banged on the door violently. The force exerted from his fist banging on the door made the entire apartment shake. Someone eventually opened the door. I peered through a little more to get a better view. To my surprise, I saw a very familiar face open the door.

It was the woman from a few days ago, the woman who was being yelled at by Lidiya. The woman that I felt I loved. The man, standing like a skyscraper over her, spoke in a deep, serious tone of voice.

"Let me in now."

The woman's eyes darted around, as if unsure of herself. She then let the man inside her apartment. As he walked past her, she saw me looking at her through the crack in the door. I immediately shut my door. I was feeling nervous. And who was that guy? What did he want with her?

I tried to stay calm, struggling to control my beating heart. Minutes later, I heard noises from the room across the hallway. Loud, angry yelling. The voices of a man and a woman, and they were screaming at each other. It was mostly the man yelling. Slowly, I walked out of my room and up to the door of the woman's room to hear the voices better. Then, I heard a loud crash, and the sound of the woman crying and screaming. I figured she was being attacked by that man. I got angry. I still had no idea who this woman was, but somehow I felt like I really cared about her.

I backed up as far as I could from my neighbor's door and centered myself to aim my foot at the lock. I took a step back and leaned in. I made my running start as fast as could. I stomped on my left foot a couple feet from the door and, with all my strength, I drove my right heel into the door near the knob. It didn't budge. I tried again, it was no use. I was quickly getting annoyed. Knowing she was in danger only made me stronger. More screams from the woman came from inside. That was the final catalyst. I kicked once more with all my might. The door cracked and flung open. I was face to face with the man.

His hands were clenched in fists with blood on the knuckles. In his fists was a large piece of ripped cloth. The woman was down on the ground with a black eye and a bloody lip. With most of her shirt torn off and her chest exposed, she was shaking with fear on the ground, crying and screaming.

I stood robustly in the doorway and ordered the man, "Get away from her!"

The man turned around and yelled, "Mind your own damn business!"

I was ready to attack. The man came at me with speed and strength. Grabbing at my shirt collar with his left hand, he swung a right hook to my head. The moment he hit me, my head rattled with pain from the force of his punch, but that didn't stop me. I raised my foot and kicked the man in the chest, forcefully separating us from each other.

We ran at each other and collided with our arms against our shoulders. The two of us were violently pushing each other into the walls of the apartment. The man then pushed me into a kitchen counter top on the other side of the room. His face was red with rage, nostrils flaring and eyes flashing. I noticed on the other side of the kitchen counter there was a large knife. I quickly picked up the knife and drew it out in front of the man. I threatened him fearlessly.

"Don't make me have to kill you! Get out now!" I said as I stood in between him and the woman with my knife pointed at him.

The man's attitude changed. He was scared at first, but then anger filled him again. He backed away toward the door and away from me and the woman.

"You'd better have eyes on the back of your heads! You're both dead!" he screamed threateningly as he ran away and out of the apartment.

I drew out my breath to finally calm down. I lowered the knife down to my side. Then I turned to the woman and offered my hand out to her.

"Are you okay?" I asked.

"Yeah, I am. Thanks."

"What's your name?" I asked.

"Violeta."

"I'm Hossan. Who was that guy?" I asked while I put the knife back onto the kitchen counter.

At first, she hesitated to answer. "He's just this guy I owe money to. He's part of a gang. I've got some debt with them because I've...," she said, unsure of herself.

"What?" I asked. She pointed over to a table over to the side.

"It's bad," she said as her voice began to shake.

"What is it?"

"I owe them money for that," Violeta said with her head down and eyes staring into the ground.

What she was pointing at were syringes and a small plastic bag holding drugs inside. The syringes had some sort of dark-colored gunk stuck to the inside. I looked around the room. It was filthy, and I only just began to notice the smell that lingered. There was trash everywhere, stains on the walls, and everything was dusty. It was as if the room were diseased or something. I then turned to Violeta, and saw a tear fall down from her eye.

"Why don't you just stop using? Have you ever at least tried to?"

"You don't get it! That's not possible! If I stop I'm gonna die!" Violeta said as she took a seat in a nearby chair, then started to cry. I tried to comfort her by putting my arm around her shoulder but then she pushed my arm away.

"Don't touch me! I'm disgusting!" Violeta said as she cried even more.

I looked around and found a shirt lying on the floor. I handed it to Violeta.

"Thanks," she said as she took the shirt and threw it on herself.

I then had an idea. I knew what I had to do. I knelt down to eye level with her.

"How about I try to help you get over this stuff," I proposed.

She started to lift her head up and stopped crying.

"What are you talking about?" she asked as she tried to wipe the tears off of her face.

"What I'm saying is that I want to help you get over the drugs. I'll come by here every morning to check up on you to see how you're doing. I'll also help you fix up the place."

"You'd do that for me?"

"Of course. It'd be inhuman to just leave you like this. I'll even protect you from those scumbag gangsters," I said confidently.

"Thanks," Violeta said as she stood up.

"First, we've got to get rid of this stuff," I said while pointing to the syringes and drugs. Violeta hesitated for a moment, and she spoke again.

"Okay. Let's do it," she said, sounding determined.

Just from the look on her face, I could tell that she was. I walked over to the syringes and drugs and picked them up.

"Where's the bathroom?" I asked. Violeta pointed to a door over to her side.

"Over there."

"Follow me," I said as I opened the door.

Violeta followed me. "You're going to throw this stuff into the toilet and flush it all down. Okay?" I explained.

Violeta nodded her head in response. I opened up the bag of drugs. It looked like brown dust, mostly. I sealed the bag up, and handed it to Violeta. I stood back so Violeta was in front of the toilet.

"Go ahead," I said, trying to support Violeta but also compelling her.

Violeta walked up to the toilet slowly. She held the bag over the toilet, pinching the corner. She was frozen in place. She reached her hand out to the handle but couldn't pull it. She was hesitant, unsure.

"You can do it," I said to try to motivate her.

Violeta took a deep breath, then dropped the heroin into the toilet. Violeta watched the bag float around in the toilet water. She took another deep breath, and reached her hand out to the handle. She grasped it tightly, and pulled down on it. The drugs swirled down the toilet. When she turned around, I saw her smile. It was like an enormous weight was just lifted off of her shoulders. She's just so beautiful.

"Now, let's get rid of these," I said as I held up the syringes. Violeta followed me out of the apartment. We walked out onto the sidewalk, and stood under a lamppost. I put one of the syringes onto the ground.

"Just follow my lead," I said to Violeta.

I raised my foot up and stomped down onto the syringe. The glass broke into different pieces, rendering it useless.

"Now you do it," I said as I put another syringe on the ground.

She looked down at the syringe and then stomped on it, hard. When it broke apart, Violeta smiled again. It was easy to see that made Violeta happy. I put another syringe on the ground. She stomped down on it again. Now Violeta started laughing. It was like music to my ears. Soon enough, even I joined in laughing. As people walked by, they looked at us weirdly. But I didn't mind. I was having too much fun.

"C'mon. Put another one down!" Violeta said as she happily laughed.

"Alright!" I responded. I reached for another syringe but there was nothing there.

"Oh, I think that was the last one," I said. Violeta then spoke.

"Oh well. It was fun though, right?" she said as she put on a wide smile on her face.

"Yeah. Yeah it was," I said, gazing into each other's eyes, laughing like crazy people.

"C'mon. Let's get back inside," I said as I walked to the main door of the apartment. Later on, we both said our goodbyes and went to sleep.

The next day, I checked up on Violeta, to see how she was doing before I went to work. I walked to her door and knocked. Violeta opened the door with a face of happiness. However her face still looked broken from the heroin and the gangster that visited her last night.

"Hey, Hossan. Nice to see you again," she said with a warm smile. I responded, by smiling with her. "Nice to see you, too. Can I come in?"

"Come on in," said Violeta.

I looked around the apartment and I was very surprised. Immediately, I noticed that the inside of Violeta's apartment looked much neater and tidier than the last time I was here; everything looked spotless.

"Did you... clean all of this by yourself?" I asked still surprised.

"Yeah, I did," she said as she spotted a piece of trash on the ground she had missed.

"It only took me an hour or so." Violeta then quickly threw away the trash into a garbage can.

"I'm really surprised. You look like you really changed," I said.

"You think so?" Violeta said with a warm smile.

"Definitely," I responded.

"Well, I guess you can take care of yourself for now. I'll see you later," I said as I walked to the door.

"Wait, where are you going?" Violeta asked as she grabbed onto my shoulder.

I turned around and said, "I'm just going to work."

Violeta responded simply with "Oh," as she sighed.

Just before I left, Violeta hugged me from behind in surprise. "Bye." She said as she released me.

"Bye." I said before leaving.

Throughout my work day I repeatedly dosed off. Of course I was thinking about Violeta. I was thinking about what she might be doing right now. My co-worker, Bartek, snapped me out of my daydreaming after calling my name over and over again.

"Hey, you okay?" Bartek asked.

"I'm fine. I was just thinking of someone," I responded.

"Oh, someone special?" Bartek asked.

"Yeah, you could say that," I said.

"Who is she?" Bartek asked, now sounding more interested.

"How do you even know it's a girl?" I asked, confused.

"There's always a girl in these types of things. I think you should ask her out!" Bartek said enthusiastically.

"You think so?"

"Of course. But it's all up to you," Bartek said as he went back to work.

Thinking about what Bartek said, I kept mopping the same floor near the same ad as the other day.

"You are amazing!" The advertisement spoke. "You can do anything in the world!" The Perfect continued to say.

The advertisement zoomed out and text to show the company logo.

"Check out our new collection later this month!" The Perfect said, posing to show off her new clothes.

From that day forward, I checked up on Violeta to see how she was doing. Each and every day she looked better and better. Before, she would rob people for money. But now, she had a job. Violeta managed to find work as a cashier in a convenience store. It wasn't much, but the pay was alright and I was extremely proud of her. It was at least enough to buy furniture. The last time I checked on her, I saw that she bought a new couch and a new TV. Of course, I kept on buying the lottery tickets periodically.

The next time we both had a day off, I decided to take her out. I saved up enough money, all I had to do was ask. I was absolutely paralyzed when I asked her out but luckily she said yes. At noon, I walked to Violeta's door to begin our day together. She opened the door and to my absolute awe, she looked amazing compared to how she was before. It was unbelievable that after just a few weeks Violeta had completely changed.

"Are you ready to go?" I asked.

"Sure. Just give me a second," she said as she grabbed her handbag.

The handbag she carried was new as well as her clothes, bought with money from her new job. I insisted that she use the money to treat herself before dealing with the Devilmen.

"Okay. So, where are we going?" Violeta asked.

"You'll see. It's somewhere really nice," I said as we left the apartment.

We walk about five blocks down from the apartment and arrive at a restaurant that I'd scoped out the week before. It was relatively new and they cooked pretty much all of their food on the grill. What I really loved about the place was that there was a constant smell of delicious food that filled the whole block.

"I've never been here before but it smells great," Violeta said as we stepped inside.

"Hello!" A waitress said, greeting us. "Two?" She asked, pointing to us."

"Yes," I replied.

The waitress directed us to a table where we took our seats and immediately looked at the menus.

"What do you think of the place?" I asked.

"It's nice," Violeta replied, bobbing her head.

We both searched through the menus for something good to eat. The selection was limited to just ten items. When I scoped the place out the week before, I got to see the menu and already planned out what to get for myself. I looked down at the menu and found the dish I wanted. A chicken dish complete with sauces and potatoes labeled on the menu as only *Chicken and Potatoes*. I kept the menu open to pretend that I was still trying to decide.

"Do you know what you want?" I asked Violeta.

"Yeah," Violeta said as she closed her menu.

A waiter soon came over to our table with a notepad in his hands.

"What would you like?" The waiter asked.

"I'd like the chicken and potatoes, please," I said.

"Okay…" The waiter said as he quickly wrote down the order. He then turned to Violeta. "What would you like?"

"I'd like the spicy pork kebabs," Violeta replied.

I looked down at what Violeta ordered. Pork kebabs with pepper, drizzled in spicy sauces.

"Would you like anything to drink?" The waiter asked.

"Just water," I said. As the waiter took our menus away, I turned to Violeta. "Is that okay with you?" I asked. Violeta nodded her head and the waiter left us.

I spent the last few days planning out what kind of questions to ask Violeta to keep her happy and entertained.

"So you like spicy food?" I asked, carefully considering what to say.

"Yeah. I can handle it," Violeta confidently stated.

"Okay. You like pork, too?"

"I like all types of meat. I could never eat liver, though," Violeta said, smiling.

"Why not? Liver is supposed to be good for you."

"I just think it's gross."

We both laughed at that. The waiter then came over with our waters. He placed the glasses of water to our sides. It gave me time to think of another question to ask to keep the conversation going.

"Can you cook?" I asked.

Violeta shook her head. "Nah. I could never cook. Wait, can you!?" She asked excitedly.

"I can boil water..." I jokingly said.

We both chuckled as I asked my next question.

"What else don't you like to eat besides liver?"

"I guess any kind of boiled vegetables," Violeta replied after giving it some thought. I nodded my head in agreement.

"I never really liked peppers," I said.

"Yeah," Violeta said, nodding in agreement.

The waiter soon came back to our table with our food in his hands. The smells of the food within the restaurant were difficult to discern between them until they were right in front of me. The waiter placed the chicken and potatoes in front of me and the pork kebabs in front of Violeta.

"Would you like anything else?" The waiter asked.

"No, thank you," I replied.

I picked up my fork and knife and immediately started cutting into the chicken. I stuffed the first piece into my mouth and it was incredible. Violeta picked up the first kebab and bit off the pork piece by piece.

"It's good, right?" I asked.

"Mhm," Violeta muttered as she chewed.

As I moved between the chicken and potatoes, Violeta asked, "Can I try?"

"Sure," I replied, cutting a piece of the chicken and placing it on her plate. Violeta quickly devoured it whole.

"That's really good," she said, still chewing.

"Let me try some of the pork," I said, pointing to Violeta's kebabs.

As Violeta passed me a kebab, some of the sauce dripped off onto the table. The sauce was bright red and mixed with black pepper to increase the spice. I took one bite and I instantly felt the spiciness of the kebab. After a couple of seconds, the spice of the sauce turned to be a little bit sweeter. I soon decided enough was enough and took a big gulp of water to try and wash down the spice.

"Too spicy, huh?" Violeta laughed, being able to easily see that I was in distress. The water failed to get rid of the burning spiciness and I turned to keep eating the chicken and potatoes to help cover it up.

I paid for the food and we headed to the next part of our day together.

"Where are we going?" Violeta asked.

"It's somewhere nice. You'll see."

When we finally arrived to the place I wanted to show Violeta, her surprise was at the same level of her confusion.

"The park? Why are we at the park?"

"Because I want to show you something amazing," I said.

I grabbed Violeta's hand and we headed up to the tallest hill in the park.

"So what did you want to show me?" Violeta asked. When we finally got to the top of the hill, I pointed to the view of Alpha city.

"That," I said, letting Violeta take in the view

"Well, what do you think?" I asked.

"It's a great view," Violeta complimented.

"Yeah. It's pretty amazing," I said. "It's a lot better when it gets dark because then you can see all the lights and everything. And you know, someday I'm thinking of living there in Alpha city. It's been my dream since I was little."

"Wait. What'll happen to me?" Violeta asked.

"What do you mean what'll happen? Are you telling me that you can't take care of yourself?"

"I can, but it's because of you that I've stopped using. What if when you leave, you won't be able to see me?" I was surprised when she said that.

I smiled, and spoke. "You don't have to worry about anything. I'm always gonna be here for you."

"I just don't want you to go."

Nobody had ever told me that before. I didn't know how to respond. Almost without thought, I wrapped my arm around Violeta's shoulders and pulled her for a tight embrace. We stood there in each other's arms. I felt like we were on top of the world. After a couple of minutes of standing around, I thought we'd spent enough time there.

"C'mon let's go." Violeta followed me out of the park.

She asked as we left, sounding obviously excited, "Where are we going now?"

"I don't know. We'll find something interesting," I replied.

At this point, I wouldn't say that we were dating or anything. But I think we were definitely getting closer. Now I just had to figure out what to do for the next couple of hours.

Moments later, we heard a voice call out to us.

"Hey! It's them!"

At first, we weren't sure who the person was calling out to until he came right up us and stopped us on the sidewalk.

"They're here!" The guy called out. Then, a large group of guys followed behind the man. There were at least seven men besides him. A slightly familiar face appeared from the crowd. Though he may be more familiar to Violeta, I immediately recognized him as the guy who attacked Violeta. He tried to approach us. I immediately flung my arm out in front of the man, in order to create distance between him and Violeta.

"What do you want!?"

I demanded an answer while trying to defend Violeta. He angrily yelled in our faces with the same tone and overall look as when we last faced him.

"I want my damn money!"

Violeta shrank with fear at the yelling. Out of nowhere, the voice of another man called out.

"Calm down. I think we can work something out here." The man's voice settled down the attacker.

The man stepped forward past the attacker and introduced himself.

"My name's Dritan. Nice to meet 'cha." He was a tall, slender man.

He wore dark leather clothes and had tattoos all over his neck and hands. He had pale white skin, like the Perfects, and wore a wide smile across his face that looked purely unnatural.

"I'm the leader of my gang here. We're the Devilmen. There's plenty of other guys trying to make a name for themselves..." Dritan paused to light a cigarette. "But we own the drug game here in good ol' Roderic," he bragged.

"Your girlfriend there owes me and my partners a lot of money. And we're a very impatient bunch. And, if you don't want to pay with money, we can find another way for your little girlfriend to pay. She could definitely pay all of us very well," Dritan said with a wicked smile. His eyes scanned Violeta's body from top to bottom.

I felt sick to my stomach every time Dritan spoke. His calm voice, coupled with his unnatural, almost disturbing smile made my skin crawl. He suddenly reached for his pocket.

"So... why don't you just surrender right now, and we'll make this as painless as possible?" Dritan said as he revealed a switch-blade knife. As Dritan flipped open the blade, the other gang members pulled out pistols. I had no idea what to do. I just did the first thing to come to my mind. RUN.

I grabbed onto Violeta's arm and ran as fast as I could. I ran so fast I was practically dragging her behind me. I tried to let her catch up but I really didn't want to wait.

"After 'em!" yelled one of the gangsters.

I have no idea where I was going. I was running into people on the sidewalk aimlessly as we were being chased by the gangsters. They weren't shooting at us or anything. Why? Maybe they wanted all of the money we had. Or maybe they wanted to make an example out of us to show exactly what it's like to have debt with these gangs. Dammit, these thoughts weren't getting me anywhere.

I saw a fence that led into an alleyway just up ahead.

"This way!" I yelled.

I helped Violeta over the fence before I climbed over. We quickly run for our lives through the alleyway over to a ladder for the fire escape. I climbed up first and Violeta followed. The gangsters quickly jumped over the fence and tried to get to the ladder as fast as possible. As Violeta was midway up the ladder, one of the gangsters grabbed onto her leg. Violeta reacted with fear first, and then action. Violeta repeatedly kicked the gangster in the face. The gangster had enough and let go of the ladder, coming down on the head of another gang member standing on the ground.

We climbed up as fast as possible and came upon an open apartment window and jumped inside. The gangsters were mere seconds away from catching us. We opened the door to this apartment and found ourselves in the hallway. A few doors down, there was a man opening the door to his own apartment. We quickly ran over to his door. I shoved the man out of the way as we ran inside.

"Sorry," I said, feeling bad for him.

Outside in the hallway, the gangsters had made up more ground.

"In there!" One of them said, pointing to the apartment door Violeta and I had gone through.

"This way!" I said to Violeta as I opened a window in the apartment.

I climbed through onto the platform of another fire escape. Violeta followed. Just as she was about to climb out onto the fire escape platform, one of the gangsters caught onto her handbag. These guys were much faster than I'd thought.

The gangster tugged harder on the bag, and the strap started to tear. Eventually, the strap broke completely and Violeta was free, but at the expense of her handbag. Violeta barely seemed to notice that she had lost it with the gangsters chasing us. We then climbed down the ladder of the fire escape and found ourselves on the sidewalk again. There was a fruit stand on the sidewalk under the fire escape. In the middle of the street there was a street performer juggling torches. There was a massive amount of people crowding around the performer. It was almost impossible for me and Violeta to try and cut through all of the spectators.

They were relentless. One of the gangsters jumped down from the platform of the fire escape in order to make it down faster. He crash landed on top of the fruit stand on the sidewalk. The other gangsters climbed down the ladder to get to the sidewalk. Dritan, however, jumped down from the fire escape platform. He carelessly used the body of the gangster who had fallen to break his fall. As we were carefully making our way through the crowd, the gangsters were pushing and shoving their way through. One of them who was pushing through yelled out to the people in front of him, "Get out of the damn way already!"

A gargantuan man, and others, turned around and faced the gangsters.

"What the hell is your problem!?" he said as he grabbed onto the gangster's shirt collar to lift him up.

"Hey! Don't fuck with us!" yelled one of the gangsters as he clocked the man in the face. The fighting spread like a fire, engulfing everyone around in a hurricane of fists. In the middle of the chaos, Violeta and I broke away from the crowd and ran down the street.

"They're getting away!" Dritan yelled angrily. He could see the situation was only getting worse. He pulled aside one of the Devilmen gangsters and stole his pistol. Dritan fired several shots into the air. All of the people screamed and everyone immediately ran like terrified mice. The street was eventually clear and the fighting had stopped.

We'd made our escape. The Devilmen were left in the streets confused, exhausted, and irritated at the fact that they had failed to capture us.

"Dammit! They got away!" Dritan yelled angrily. His evil, twisted smile had been wiped off his face by his own frustration. Dritan turned around and spotted a handbag in the hands of one of the Devilmen.

"Hey, what's that?" Dritan asked the gangster.

"Oh yeah, I snatched it off of that bitch we were chasing," the gangster explained.

"Hand it over," Dritan said as he held out his hand. The man immediately handed over the handbag to Dritan.

"Okay, let's see," Dritan said as he rummaged through the bag.

"What are you looking for?" The other gangsters asked.

"Ah, here it is," he said as he pulled out Violeta's apartment key.

"I'm guessing this the key to her apartment. See, look, the address is on the back, too," Dritan said, holding up the key and reading the address.

"Alright, let's go!" Dritan ordered as they headed to the apartment.

Meanwhile, Violeta and I made our way into a crowded market in order to lose the gangsters.

"I think they're gone. We're alright now," I said.

I turned to Violeta and saw that she had her head down.

"Hey, what's the matter?" I asked.

"No, it's just... I don't want to get you involved in this kind of stuff with me. I just don't want you to get hurt," Violeta said. She looked as if she were on the verge of tears.

"Don't worry about me. I'll be alright," I said. "Why don't we just walk around for a while? It'll calm us down. Alright?" Violeta agreed, and we walked aimlessly to try to kill time and hopefully avoid the Devilmen gangsters.

I tried to calm her down as best as I could throughout the whole day. I could tell that she never wanted any of this to happen to her. I was proud to see that she'd turned her life around, or at least she was trying to.

It was getting really dark, so we both decided to head back to the apartment. On the way there, I stopped at a machine to buy another lottery ticket. The numbers were 11, 5, 7, 3, and 42.

"Why do you keep buying those?" Violeta asked as she watched me take the ticket. I thought about it for a little bit.

"To be honest, I'm not exactly too sure anymore." I turned to Violeta and said, "You wanna know something? Ever since I met you, I think I cared more about you than the lottery or anything."

I then walked up closer to her. "Tell you what. This is the last time I'm buying these lottery tickets, okay? I'm happy just where I am," I said with a warm smile. Violeta smiled back and nodded. We then hugged each other as we walked into the apartment.

I unlocked the front door of the apartment and Violeta and I walked up the stairs to our rooms. When we got to the top of the stairs, we saw that Violeta's door was wide open.

"That's weird. I remember locking the door when I left." When she walked into her room, she was shocked. She covered her mouth with her hand and slowly sat on the ground. I went into the room to see what she saw.

Her room was in shambles. The cushions of her couch were torn open, the TV screen was smashed in, and there were bullet holes in the walls, where in black spray paint the men who did this to Violeta's apartment wrote *DON'T FUCK WITH THE DEV-ILMEN!* Those scumbags did this. I felt as if a furnace burned inside me. I felt my blood boil. I just wanted to rip their heads off!

I walked over to the door to inspect it. The door knob and lock were completely intact so they definitely didn't break in.

"How did they even get in here? Maybe they picked the lock?" I muttered to myself.

"No, I'm pretty sure they used my room key," said Violeta.

"How did they get your room key?" I asked, confused.

"While we were escaping, one of them got my handbag. I had my room key in there and they must've used it to get in," Violeta explained.

"That makes sense," I responded. I helped Violeta up to her feet.

"Well, you can't stay in here in anymore, obviously. Why don't you stay with me? Just until we get this place fixed up," I proposed.

"Are you serious?" Violeta asked, surprised.

"Of course. What? You think I'm just going to let you stay here?" I said, smiling.

The second after I said that, Violeta hugged me. She was ecstatic, thanking me over and over again. I let Violeta bring whatever was left from her room into mine.

In between her bringing in boxes of things, she brought in a photo album. I picked it up and opened it to flip through the photos. I saw pictures of a cute little girl with black hair and blue eyes holding hands with her parents. Violeta came into my room with another box.

"Okay, this is the last one," Violeta said as she set down the last box.

"Is this you?" I asked, handing Violeta the picture.

"Oh, yeah. I think I was five when this was taken."

She then pointed to two adults in one of the pictures. They were smiling, holding up each of Violeta's hands.

"Those were my parents. I always loved them, and I know they loved me, but I just needed to get out of there. They'd always be fighting, and I'd be around to see it all happen."

"Why were they fighting?" I asked.

"I don't know. I think it was money troubles. I was an addict, a thief, and I did a lot of stuff that I don't want to talk about," Violeta explained with an apparent sadness in her voice.

"It must've been hard," I added. Violeta nodded her head in response.

"Yeah but that was ages ago. What matters is what's happening right now," Violeta added. I agreed, nodding my head.

"So what about you?" Violeta asked.

"What are you talking about?" I replied.

"What about your parents? What were they like?"

I thought about the question for a little bit. I know what my answer is, it's just that I always felt uncomfortable thinking about it. I took in a deep breath and spoke.

"I never really talked to my parents. I never really spent too much time with them," I started. "One of the reasons I never talked to my parents is because as a kid, I was very independent. I'd always get out of my house and walk around Roderic. You know, explore the city."

I showed my obvious hesitation by sighing and looking down at the ground before I gave my second reason. I knew this was what bothered me most about my parents.

"The other reason... was that my parents had drug problems. They'd always be doing drugs every day. All my parents would think about was getting high. I've barely ever even seen them eat cause of how high they always got."

"Okay, stop," Violeta interrupted. "I think that's enough. You probably shouldn't think about that kind of stuff anymore."

"Yeah, you're probably right," I responded. Violeta then rested her head on my shoulder.

"I think we should go to sleep soon."

I agreed. It was late, and I was tired. I wasn't just tired because it was late. I was tired of all that had happened. I was tired of the gangs, the drugs, the crime, and all of the nonsense that went with it all. I'm sure Violeta was tired of all of it as well.

Just before I went to sleep, I thought of watching a little TV.

"Hold on, I just want to check something really quick," I said as I turned the TV on.

Immediately after I turn on the TV, a new music video played. A bunch of half-naked Perfects danced around each other with Gisele Williams in the focus.

"Do you like the Perfects?" Violeta asked me.

"Of course I do. Who doesn't?" I responded.

At first, Violeta hesitated to reply. But her tone of voice when replying reflected a sense of frustration with my answer.

"Well, I don't. I think they're all really just a bunch of snobby pricks."

"What! How can you even say that!?" I said, in complete disbelief. "They're all perfect! That's why they're called the Perfects!" I retorted.

"Yeah, but I mean, what else do they do besides party? All they care about is partying. We work our fingers to the bone ever hour of every day of every year. We do all that to make the same amount of money that could feed families here but would probably just be pocket change to the Perfects! Like I said, the Perfects are all just a bunch of snobby pricks. All they want to do is fuck, and get fucked up," Violeta finished.

I calmed down, and took in a deep breath. "Yeah, you're probably right."

"Why do you like them so much?" Violeta asked.

I thought about it for a little bit, and was left with no real answers that came to mind.

"To be honest, I really don't know. I just know that I don't like being a human. Ever since I can remember, all I ever wanted was something better in my life and I thought that was to be a Perfect."

"Well, maybe you don't need to be like them. I mean, I'm here with you." I instantly felt much happier when she said that. All previous bad thoughts flooded out of my head in that instant.

"Yeah, you're right. I'm glad to have you with me," I said.

"Me too," Violeta replied.

We hugged, but I wanted to kiss her. I kept thinking about how it'd feel to kiss Violeta as she laid on the covers and I'd just caress her body as I'd continue kissing her. But we didn't. Violeta laid on her side with her back to me. I laid down next to her and pulled the covers over us. I heard Violeta take a deep breath as she grabbed some of the covers for herself.

I had my arms under the covers just behind her back. I stretched my arms over and around Violeta's hips. I did it as slowly as I could, expecting that she'd push my arms away. But by the time my arms completely wrapped around her hips, I knew Violeta didn't mind at all. Luckily, we quickly went to sleep before the thundering noise of the curfew siren echoed through the city.

I woke up in a haze. I had a weird dream where I woke up alone in my bed. I was in a place where everything around me, even the sky, was white. I could barely move, and Violeta was gone. I then heard a beautiful voice come from the sky. A beautiful Perfect woman descended down to me as she sang a tune in her gorgeous voice. She floated above me and stretched her arms around me. She pulled me up from my bed and I was in the air. I only kept moving up. I looked to my side and saw the ground itself was nearly out of sight from my peripheral. I was terrified. Suddenly, the Perfect woman put her palms on my cheeks and pushed around my head to make me face forward. Our eyes were locked together. I remember her eyes were staring into mine as if in some sort of trance. Soon after, I woke up in my room in a sweat with Violeta next to me. I nudged her until she woke up.

"Good morning," Violeta said.

"Good morning. How did you sleep?" I replied.

"I slept well. I'm going to make us breakfast," I said as I got up from the bed.

"What are we having?"

"Eggs and toast?" I suggested. I thought it was a simple idea for breakfast.

After she got dressed, Violeta went out to buy eggs for breakfast. I didn't want her to leave in case she would get attacked again, but she insisted. I threw some of the lottery tickets into the furnace along with a match. The pile started to burn, and the furnace heated up. I thought making breakfast for her would be a nice start as I really want to welcome Violeta into staying with me. And also I usually just eat things from a convenience store for breakfast, so it's a nice change to start eating actual food for once.

I turned the TV on. The usual shows from Alpha city were being broadcast. After they finished with an episode of a reality TV show, it switched over to the host. He spoke in his normally loud and confident tone.

"All right, ladies and gentlemen! We will now be getting the numbers for the Lucky Day lottery!" He then pointed over to a Perfect girl in a bikini, the camera following. "Now, sexy Katie is going to bring out the winning numbers!" He said as the camera focused in on a bikini clad Perfect girl. A different one than before.

The number appeared on screen as she announced them. One by one, they appeared on screen. 11, 5, 7, 3, and 42. I thought about the numbers for a second after I heard them. Then a memory blasted through my head like a rocket. It struck me like a lightning bolt. I frantically started looking around the apartment for the ticket. The last ticket I bought had those numbers!

I searched through every drawer and cabinet. I looked through all of my clothes and the trash can. I insanely tried to read all of the past tickets on the ground and in the trash thinking the winner got mixed in with the others. I soon realized there was only one other place the ticket could be. The furnace. I opened the furnace and immediately felt the heat of the fire beat against my face. I saw the winning ticket in the back. I quickly reached in, grabbed the ticket, and ripped my arm out. I had burned my hand a little bit, but I didn't care. I read the ticket; it was the exact same numbers in the exact same combination.

I quickly got dressed. I packed my bags with all of my clothes and personal belongings. With the ticket in my hand and my bags in the other, I bolted out the door. When I got out of the door, I passed Violeta with a bag of groceries in her hand. I barely noticed her in my frantic state of mind. I was halfway down the stairs when I realized that I'd passed Violeta. I paused. At first, Violeta looked surprised at me. Then she saw me holding my bag in one hand and the ticket in another. She knew exactly what was happening, and Violeta spoke in a cold tone of voice.

"Congratulations."

I could feel my guilt begin to crush my soul like a car compactor. I thought about how this is so incredibly, extremely selfish and that I should stay with her. But when is this kind of opportunity going to happen to me again? I won the lottery twice! The planets must've aligned and god must've used all of his power for this to happen. If I don't take my chance now, I would never have it again. Without another thought, I left the apartment with the ticket in hand.

I rushed to Alpha city. I hid the ticket in my bag and held onto it tightly. I didn't want to take the chance of getting mugged again. So this time I made sure I took the train with the most passengers on board all the way the Alpha city. As the wheels of the train moved, I thought about all of this. Was this really the right thing to do? Was it really okay for me to leave Violeta all alone?

Before I could come up with an answer, the train stopped at the station in Alpha city. I got off and saw the towering buildings above me. My mind automatically began to fantasize about living in one of these amazing buildings. I walked over to the place where they run the Lucky Day lottery. There was a Perfect man sitting behind a counter. He extended his hand out as soon as I entered.

"May I see your ticket?" he asked.

I looked to my side and leaning against the wall was a gargantuan Perfect man. He was staring at me with such animosity. He looked like a tiger ready to pounce on its prey. I assumed he was part of the security here. Or rather maybe he's all the security this place needs. Just like all of the other Perfects, his skin was pure white and the smile of his smile mask stretched across his face.

The Perfect man sitting behind the counter asked again, sounding annoyed.

"May I see the ticket? Please."

I opened my bag and took out the ticket. All my life, I'd been working tirelessly for this. This moment, this was what everything that I'd done in my life led up to. All my regrets, all of my fears, everything that I hated would disappear soon. But I wouldn't be able to see Violeta anymore. Maybe I'd be able to catch her while she's working or something.

The second I handed the Perfect man the ticket, he scanned it with a device to confirm that it was the right ticket. He then stood up from his chair and walked.

"This way, please," he said as he opened a door to a back room. The room, just like most of the other ones in Alpha city, was all white. Inside, there was an enormous machine with a platform and a control box near it.

"Please undress. Then stand on the platform," the Perfect man instructed.

I followed his instructions and stood still on the platform. The metal platform felt so cold under my feet. He then walked over to the control box and pressed a few buttons. Suddenly, long rectangular holograms appeared around me. I took a closer look at them and saw that they were all shaped like measuring tapes. They all wrapped around my body, measuring my height, waist, arms and legs. The man collected the data and then pushed some more buttons.

"One moment, please," he said calmly.

I waited for a few seconds and suddenly the machine whirred and vibrated. I stuck my head out and realized the noise came from a box attached to the machine that looked a printer. Like it was printing out paper, a white suit was printed from the machine. The man took the suit and pushed it to me.

"Put this on," he said as he handed me the suit.

It felt very soft and fit on my body perfectly. I noticed there are holes in the suit where my arms, legs, and chest would be. The holes were surrounded with metal circles like screw holes. I looked up to the man in confusion.

"Is it supposed to be like this?" I asked, pointing to the holes.

"Of course. It's very fashionable and don't worry, it looks great on you," he said.

He then walked over to another door.

"Right in here," he said.

I saw that this room was incredibly dirty inside. The man pointed to a chamber at the end of the room.

"Get in there," he ordered. I did as he said.

When I stepped inside the chamber, the door slammed shut behind me. I assumed this was how I was going to be transformed into one of the Perfects. I saw that there were restraints on the walls.

"Put your wrists and ankles inside the restraints now," I heard the Perfect say to me. I looked up to see a small speaker in the chamber where the voice came from.

I felt a little confused about the need for restraints, but I put my wrists and ankles into them anyway and they automatically closed. A loud buzzing noise began to sound through the chamber, almost like the curfew alarm. Out of nowhere, a blinding flash of light flashed into my face, and I felt a powerful shock coarse through my body. I started to lose consciousness and my eyes were closing. Just before my eyes shut, I saw the chamber door open, and felt someone pull me out.

Suddenly, I woke up in a haze on a soft, luxurious bed, in an unbelievably luxurious apartment. I looked out the window to see that it was nighttime. The walls and floor were carpeted. It felt perfectly warm. A giant flat screen TV was on the wall in front of me. There was a deck just outside of the room that overlooked Alpha city. I felt the softness of the brand new clothes I was wearing, on top of the high-quality fabric of the bed. I then looked down at my hands and saw that they were pure white. I saw that there was a mirror across the room and I quickly jumped out of my bed, and dashed over to the mirror and I saw my smile mask on my face and the skin on body. It was all completely white. I was taller, stronger, and felt like a king.

Suddenly, a Perfect woman opened the door to my room.

"Hello. Looks like you're getting settled. I'm a nurse. I'm just here to check up on you, sir."

She was absolutely beautiful just like all of the other Perfects. She held onto a clipboard and pen to take notes.

"Now, how are you feeling?"

I responded boisterously, "I feel fucking awesome!"

"Are you enjoying your stay?" she asked.

"So far, yeah."

"Do you remember anything since your transformation?" she asked as she jotted down notes on her clipboard.

I tried to explore my mind for any memories at all, but nothing came. Then, I felt a small spark of a memory in my brain.

"Oh yeah, I do remember one thing."

The instant I said that, the nurse stopped writing on her clipboard. The smile on her mask stayed the same but she glared at me viciously.

"What exactly do you remember?" she asked.

Her tone and behavior had suddenly done a 180. It was as if she were talking to an alien.

"I remember being pulled out of the chamber. I blacked out right after, but I think that was after the transformation was over."

"Is that all?" she asked.

"Yeah. Yeah, I think that's about it," I responded.

The nurse's nice tone of voice and normal behavior returned and she wrote the last of her notes down.

"Thank you for your time, sir."

Just as she left, I stopped her. "Wait," I said.

"Why did you call me sir?" She looked surprised after hearing my question.

"Are you kidding me? It's because you're special! You're a star!" she said as she left. I'd almost forgotten. The minute a normal human is transformed into a Perfect, they become an instant celebrity.

After the nurse left the room, another Perfect entered. It was a man wearing a black blazer, black pants, and a purple shirt underneath. He had a short crew cut and wore sunglasses.

"Hey dude! How's it going!?" he yelled excitedly.

"I'm fine. Who are you?" I asked.

"I'm your manager! Name's Tony, by the way. Okay? Okay. Now, are you ready or what!?"

"Ready for what?"

"What do you mean what? Your debut appearance! We're gonna show you off on TV in like ten minutes!"

"Alright, let's go then!" I responded.

"Alright! Let's go, go, go!" he said ecstatically.

We left the room and headed down the hallway. As we headed down the hall, two Perfect girls stepped out of their room. As soon as they saw this face, they lit up with excitement. They waved to me and I waved back. We made it to the elevators and Tony hit the button to call the elevator up.

I turned to Tony and asked, "So, what are we doing?"

"Well..," Tony stopped mid speech to pull out a cigarette from his jacket pocket. "We're just gonna show you off. You know, make you look great for everyone to see. We're going to answer a couple of questions. One thing will lead to another and we'll just party after it's over. There'll be girls and champagne and everything. You're gonna love it!"

"Okay. So where are we going?" I asked as Tony puffed out a cloud of cigarette smoke.

"Somewhere close," he said.

The elevator doors opened and we stepped inside. Tony pushed a button on the control panel and we moved downward. I was still confused as to where we were going. We passed three levels going down.

"Oh yeah, I almost forgot. You've got a new identity, a whole new face and body. That means you're getting a new name."

"What is it?"

"Your new name is Jack Miller."

"Alright, but what was my old name?" Tony stopped smoking for a second.

"That doesn't matter, that was your old self, your human self. What matters now is just to look pretty. And also, don't be afraid to get a little wild. It'll turn people on when they watch you. Trust me," he explained.

I nodded my head. "Awesome."

The elevator traveled more levels down through a glass shaft. It was dark beyond the glass barrier of the elevator, but soon everything lit up. We descended towards the middle of a room the size of a stadium. There were too many Perfects to count. All of them watching from the stands, all of them cheering. There was loud music full of earth-shattering bass being blasted from all corners of the room and hundreds of cameras were watching me. I could hear from the elevator that the announcer was beginning the show. Along with the announcer's voice, I could hear the applause of the cheering fans.

The announcer spoke with a boomingly confident voice, "Alright! Everyone better listen up right here!" Most of the applause began to calm down when they heard the announcer. "As we speak, we got one of the biggest names in the world gracing us with his presence! The incredible, the outstanding megastar, Jack Miller!"

His voice echoed through the room with my name and I was deeply welcomed again with millions of thunderous cheers.

Some of the cameras even had rotors attached to them like helicopters. A few of them hovered past the elevator to get a close-up shot of me.

"It's so awesome, you know? Millions of people paying attention to you and everything you say and do," I said, looking out to thousands of cheering fans, and myself as energetic as a little kid.

"Yeah", Tony replied, sounding disinterested.

"What? You don't think so?" I asked, confused. Tony didn't reply, he simply ignored me and lit another cigarette. Smoking until the elevator stopped shortly.

"Let's go," he ordered.

The elevator doors opened and there was a wide white stage in front of us. Tony and I stepped out of the elevator and walked. As we walked, Tony and I waved to the millions of cheering fans. In the middle of the stage were two people. A Perfect man who looked strongly built and wore a black tank top and shorts, and another, a

Perfect woman with a curvy body, wearing a tiny black dress. The both of them were sitting in large soft chairs and next to them were two more chairs reserved for me and Tony.

Tony and I sat down in the empty chairs and the show started.

"Hey! Mark here! Here with me to my side is the beautiful, super sexy Alexis!" he said as he introduced Alexis.

"Heeeey!" Alexis happily greeted the cameras as they flew by.

With the camera about to pan over to my face, Mark spoke again, bolstering the confidence in his voice.

"We're here with celeb icon, the living legend, the god, Jack Miller, everybody!" Everyone in the stands cheered once more before Mark continued.

"Before he won, Jack was just a pathetic little human. But then we put him in the light! We made him into... a megastar! And once he became a megastar, he instantly outclassed and humiliated his rivals! We turned him from a pathetic little human into a class A citizen! A megastar!"

Tony waved to the hovering helicopter cameras as they passed by. I stuck my middle finger out to the cameras. It was all for the entertainment. The audience cheered even louder when they heard my name and saw my face.

"So, how would you describe your time so far?" Alexis asked me.

I answered in my own loud, confident tone of voice.

"Aw, man, it's been real crazy so far. I'm so glad I'm here. I'd like to take a moment to thank the Lord, thank God for all he's done for me!"

The crowd's cheers echoed with my answer.

"Could you give some advice to our viewers? Maybe on how they can be more like you?"

"Damn, you know, I was in the ghetto for a hell of a long time. But I knew that I was born to be a winner, born to be famous but most of all... born to be a Perfect! And you know what, I was like a parasite or something, some piece of shit. And you know what I did? I bought those fuckin' tickets! So for all the little humans watching, go out and buy those fuckin' tickets! I won the Lucky

Day lottery, and now just look at me! Look at me now!" I said proudly. I laughed, feeling confident. The audience cheered loudly.

Now living in Hossan's apartment, Violeta watched Jack's show on TV. It's only been a few days since Hossan left but to her it feels like years. Violeta couldn't recognize Hossan at all as Jack. Violeta can't make sense of why Hossan decided to leave. Confused, Violeta put her head into her arms as tears began to roll down her face. Crying, she pushed into her arm the needle of a syringe with black gunk stuck to the inside.

The show kept switching between prerecorded interviews with different Perfects.

"What do you think about Jack Miller?" An interviewer asked, stopping two random Perfects on the street.

"He's just like so cool and such an inspiration," one of the Perfects answered. His friend standing next to him added, "Yeah, like, he's really inspired all of us."

The questions kept on rolling from the hosts. And after each answer that I gave, the audience cheered even louder. I felt unstoppable. The show then started to wind down.

"Okay, everyone, looks like we're outta time! Stay tuned for more celebrity news coming up next! We're also gonna show you the trailer for the new movie all about Jack's rise to fame, *I Wanna Be a Megastar!* See you again tomorrow!" Mark finished.

And with that, the show ended. The cameras stopped rolling and we made our exit.

"Alright, let's go!" Tony ordered as he and I walked off the stage.

"Where to now?" I asked.

"We're going to the party!" Tony yelled excitedly as we walked out of the building.

Outside of the building was a long red carpet leading out to a limousine. As Tony and I walked, fans rushed to try to get their hands on me and pushed me to sign autographs for them. The only things separating us from them were velvet rope and giant security guards. Flashes from hundreds of cameras brightened the night sky. They would've blinded anyone. Luckily, I had a pair of sunglasses on. The chauffeur opened the door for us. Tony climbed inside first. Before we left I waved to the crowd one last time as I heard their roaring cheers.

In the limo, Tony pulled open the center cushion to reveal a container of ice and a small compartment for glasses. Tony pulled out a bottle of champagne from the ice and poured a glass of champagne for me and for himself. He passed the glass over to me.

"To us!" he said as he raised the glass up high.

I raised mine as well. We both clinked our glasses and took sipped the champagne. It was like drinking liquid gold. I felt pretty damn amazing. I felt so alive and confident that I opened up the sunroof above me and stuck my head out. I saw the lights of Alpha city pass by me like a thousand comets.

"WOOOO! Look at me! Look at me!" I yelled out into the night sky with my fists in the air.

I climbed back into the limousine. Tony lit up another cigarette and he blew out some smoke out through the sunroof.

"Where's the party?" I asked.

"It's at your place," Tony replied.

"Wait, I thought that other place we came from was my place," I said, confused.

"No, man. That was just one of the green rooms," Tony explained.

The car slowed down to a crawl as we turned into the driveway.

"We're here," the chauffeur, another Perfect, announced as he parked the car.

"Alright, let's go!" Tony said as he blasted the doors open and stepped out with grace.

To my amazement, I saw an enormous building standing tall in front of me with lights as bright as the sun. The building itself was slightly curved to give a modern look, including a long angular roof and deck platforms. A narrow brook pathway lined with small lights up to the front steps cut through a perfectly manicured lawn. The cherry on top, a giant fountain out front.

"Is this the place?" I asked, barely able to contain myself.

"Yup. It's all yours," Tony said. Fans and paparazzi rushed over to take pictures of me but security stopped them in their tracks.

"Okay, everyone, make a path!" The guards said as they pushed the photographers back. There were tons of people driving up to my place, all in sports cars and appropriately dressed in only the trendiest of clothes.

As I stepped inside, I was instantly welcomed with smiles and hugs from the girls and high-fives and fist bumps from the guys.

Most guys came wearing high end clothes but some decided to arrive dressed in baggy shorts and tank tops which I was cool with. We all danced to loud, bass-driven songs. I made my way over to a huge couch and coffee table and the people already sitting there welcomed me. All that was on the table was an array of drugs and liquor around a container with a nozzle attached to it. A lot like an iv drip. A few more girls came over to sit near me. One of them made her way to sit right on my crotch. A guy sitting near us took the device off the table and scooped up the drugs and alcohol to pour into the jar. The guy swished it around like he was making a cocktail and he motioned for me to give him my arm. I was up for anything so reached out my arm. The girl sitting on my lap pushed my arm to him harder. With the girl holding my arm up, the guy stuffed the nozzle into one of the holes on my arm meant for pumping Formula H and the concoction was immediately drained into my arm.

The feeling of the drugs and alcohol sweeping through my body was euphoric to say the least. It was so intense that I could barely control myself. I saw there were more people dancing outside by the pool. I ran outside to the pool, and ripped off all of my clothes. The other Perfects cheered when they saw me and I jumped into the pool with everyone else. The feeling of drugs and alcohol intensified. I pushed my head through the water and saw everyone around the edge of the pool clapping and cheering for me.

"Get in here!" I yelled out to everyone as I motioned for them to come join me.

Everyone stripped down and jumped in as we danced through the rest of the night in a hurricane of drugs, tits, and alcohol.

The next morning, I could barely open my eyes, as if they were sewn shut. When I could finally open my eyes, I found my once luxurious and extravagant home turned upside down into a wasteland.

"Aw, shit, what happened?" I said, confused and surveying the destruction.

My headache felt like my brains were violently shaking in my skull. I pulled some girl's panties off my head. All I had on was my underwear and a torn up t-shirt with a bunch of different stains on it. It wasn't even my shirt. I stood up, finding that I had slept on top of some naked girl who reeked of alcohol. I looked around and saw mountains of empty cups and bottles. What looked like the aftermath of a war was tons of Perfects passed out around the house. I ignored the bodies and sidestepped my way to my bedroom, avoiding puddles of booze and more bodies.

I think if I can get upstairs to by bedroom, I can get some better sleep. Hopefully, I won't suddenly remember any regretful actions from the night before. Feeling parched after a night of partying, I filled myself a glass of water before making my way upstairs.

Actually walking up the stairs feels like trying to march up a mountain. I felt like I was climbing the side of a skyscraper, feeling weaker and more nauseous with each step. Finally getting up to my room, I flung open the door. The mere sound of the door hitting the wall was more than enough to worsen my headache.

My bedroom was just as luxurious as the rest of my house. Surprisingly, there wasn't anyone passed out in my room. They probably thought that it'd be a bad idea to piss me off by crashing in my room. Smart.

I can hear my bed calling for me to rest on its softness. I looked past the bed and saw the balcony which overlooked my property. I decided to get some fresh air before going back to sleep. I stumbled over to the glass door to the balcony and opened it to be blasted with fresh air. I stepped out onto the balcony and looked over the railing. The sight outside was similar to the inside. People had parked their sports cars on the front lawn. Clothes, bottles of alcohol, and more hungover bodies were strewn around the front lawn. I sighed, feeling ready to go to sleep as I took a sip of the water.

I looked further past the tall buildings and could see something in the distance that contrasted with the rest of the view. It was Roderic.

My ears began ringing like an alarm. I felt dizzy. I could barely keep my balance and everything turned white. Suddenly, a distant memory flashed into my head. It was so overwhelming that I let the glass of water slip out of my hands and shatter on the floor. I visualized streets, a park with lots of big hills, and an apartment. What was this? I kept thinking to myself about everything, but I couldn't get it right, I had no idea what I was seeing. I tried to throw other memories at it to try and make sense of it but nothing came to mind.

I started feeling weaker and sicker than ever before. My head pounded. My body ached with so much pain that I could barely stand up. I lowered myself to sit on the ground, clutching my head, hoping it would all stop. Suddenly, I felt my skin crawl all over my body as if death was hovering over me about to lay claim to my soul. I felt something seep out of my body. I looked at my arms and legs and saw black, oily sludge flowing out of the holes for pumping in Formula H. The sludge stained my clothes and formed a puddle beneath me. It was disgusting. I felt disgusting. I assumed it was Formula H pouring out of me. If it's true then that's really bad, but I doubt this is supposed to happen to anyone anyway.

"What the hell is this shit?" I asked myself, somehow expecting an answer.

Out of nowhere, Tony came walking into the room.

"Hey, man, what's up!?" he said loudly. I was instantly knocked out by how loudly he spoke.

"Shut up!" I shouted angrily.

"Sorry, man..." Tony said. He then got closer to clearly see the black sludge all over my body.

"What the hell is happening with you!?" he asked.

"I don't know. It just started like this," I said, becoming more and more afraid of what was happening.

"Hold on..." Tony said as he reached into his coat pocket. "Here," Tony said, holding onto a pouch labeled *Formula H*.

The pouch of Formula H had a plastic nozzle on top that would fit into the holes on my body. Tony grabbed my arm, the aching pain intensified with touch. Tony stuffed the nozzle into the hold on arm and squeezed the pouch.

"What are you doing?" I asked, confused.

"Don't worry about it," Tony responded.

My feeling of weakness began to slip away. I started feeling like I could concentrate on the moment at hand.

"Wait right here. I'm gonna get some towels."

Beginning to regain my strength, I slowly stood up. I pushed myself up with the railing of the balcony, trying to get my head together, trying to remember and make sense of the memories I saw. I tried to connect it with every other bit of memory in my head but nothing came to me. Tony soon came back into the room with some towels and threw them in my direction. I caught them and immediately started wiping the black sludge off my arms and legs.

"Alright, man. Get dressed 'cause we're getting out of here."

I stripped off my clothes and wiped off the rest of the sludge before finding something to wear from the closets in my room. By the time I finished getting dressed, my hangover was totally gone. All of the pain subsided by the time I was out the door. Stepping outside, I saw that most of people were beginning to wake up and leave. I saw Tony standing by a limousine, smoking a cigarette.

"C'mon, man, let's go!" Tony called. I got inside quickly and the limousine started to drive off.

"You alright?" Tony asked.

"Yeah..." I answered. "Hey, are all those people gonna leave or what? And what about inside?"

"Don't worry," he said, puffing out some smoke. "I'll send some people over to get all that shit cleaned up," he responded casually.

"Alright. So, where are we going?" I asked.

"We're going to the music studio to get you ready. You'll be in a photoshoot with some cute girls. Sounds great, right?" he said enthusiastically.

"Yeah!" I responded, now excited by Tony's enthusiasm.

We drove into the city and eventually stopped in front of a large building like many others in Alpha city.

"Is this it?" I said, looking up at the building from inside the limo.

"Yup," Tony said as he opened the door and we stepped out onto the sidewalk.

We walked through the front door and took the elevator to the fifth floor. We walked through a hall and made our way into a large room with a bunch of high tech photography equipment. Everything was already set with a sports car in place in front of a white curtain and Perfect bikini-clad models standing around.

"Over here," Tony said, directing me to a man wearing casual clothes, talking to one of the models.

"Hey!" Tony called out to him.

Both the man and the model took immediate notice of me and looked amazed that I was there. The man had a giant, high-tech camera slung on his neck. He motioned for the model to leave as he approached us.

"Hello! My name's Sam. I'm the photographer," he said, looking straight at me and sticking open hand out to me. "It's an honor to work with you," he said.

"Yeah," I said, shaking his hand.

"Wait right here," Sam said as he left. He returned with a small pile of clothes in his hands.

"Put this on. There's a changing room just over there," he said pointing to a door on the other side of the room.

I brought the clothes into the changing room and threw them on. Black jeans, a white shirt, black leather jacket, and a belt. The clothes looked super trendy and high-end from what I could tell. I picked up the last piece before the jacket, a luxurious leather belt, and slipped it through the belt loops. When I finished putting on the belt, I admired myself in the mirror. I turned my body around to try to find the best angles for people to see me. Out of nowhere, I started to feel sick and weak.

It felt like my body was completely giving up and shutting down all at once. It almost felt like my insides were being liquefied and stirred around. I felt ice cold, my head pounded. In my head, I can see more memories. I saw hundreds of tickets around me and the inside of a shitty little apartment. None of it makes any sense. How could I know those things? I saw that some of the black sludge was starting to drip out of the holes on each of my arms. I didn't want to ruin the shoot with stained clothes. I quickly grabbed the shirt I wore on my way here and wiped it all off my arms and the rest of my body.

I try to push away these weird memories by imagining anything else. I started thinking of TV shows. I thought about the party from last night. I tried to throw as many memories around my head as fast as I could to keep me from thinking about the other memories. After about five minutes, I felt a little bit better. My head still pounded, but I went out for the shoot. I put on the leather jacket and I approached the photographer.

"I'm ready," I said.

"Great. I want you to lean on the hood of the car," Sam said, pointing over to the sports car.

I walked over to the sports car and leaned on the hood, careful not to damage the car. Sam motioned to me with his hand. The bikini models came over. They sat on the car and cuddled up to me. They sure as hell got me hard.

"Okay, nice." Sam complimented as he positioned himself for the first few shots.

The camera flashed and the first few shots were taken.

"Good… good. Get a little closer," Sam said. As soon as he said so, I was tightly sandwiched between the girls.

As more pictures were taken, I could feel myself get weaker. I just have to endure it for a little longer, I thought, and then I can go home and rest up. Just focus on the girls. Focus on Sam and Tony standing together, watching. I kept trying to think about anything else but the memories or the aching pain all over my body.

"What the fuck!?" One of the models screamed as she stood up.

Everyone, including myself, was startled and confused. The model had black sludge all over her shoulder. I then looked at my arms and saw the black sludge oozing out. The other models stood up and screamed in shock. Everyone looked at me in shock. As the models whispered to each other and Sam looked on, Tony walked up to me with another Formula H pouch in his hand.

Tony grabbed me to push the pouch into my arm. Tony grabbing my arm made the pain unbearable. I pulled my arm back and pushed Tony away. After that, I ran. I needed to get home, I can't be out here, I thought. I bolted out of the room and quickly headed for the elevator. I pressed the button to call for the elevator. Luckily, the doors opened quickly and I was in. I quickly pressed the button for the bottom floor and continued to lean against the railing inside the elevator. I could barely stand. It felt like my body was shutting down, like I could pass out at any time.

The elevator reached the bottom floor and I stumbled out. I tried to get up but it seemed impossible. I saw the front door just ahead of me, which seemed like a million miles away. I decided to crawl. The other memories came to me like a tsunami sweeping over my brain. The memories played in my head like vivid animation. I saw the face of some girl. I saw myself walking with her, talking to her, sleeping next to her. It was all about her. I put one hand ahead of me and started crawling for the door. I stopped, and saw that my hands were becoming wrinkled and gray. They felt brittle, as if disintegrating. I'm going to die here I don't leave now.

I kept crawling and crawling and crawling until I got to the door. I pulled myself up by the door knob and pushed it open. I ran out onto the sidewalk. The limo was waiting. I opened the door and jumped in. The driver saw me, and gave me a look of pure confusion.

"Just drive! Get me to my house!" I ordered.

The driver immediately put the car in gear and drove off. Meanwhile, Tony was still upstairs making a call to the Mayor of Alpha city, Michael Rollins.

"We've got a problem. He's having malfunctions in his system. I think he's actually starting to remember," Tony said, concerned. He then received orders from Michael Rollins on the other side of the line. Tony sighed as he responded.

"Yes. I understand."

Tony could see from a window in the studio that I had ridden off in the limo. He then made another call, this time to the limo driver.

"This is Tony. Specimen 245J's system has been corrupted. Crash the limo," he ordered.

The limo driver responded with, "Yes, sir."

The chauffeur then floored the gas pedal. I was pushed back by the torque and immediately thought this was way too fast.

"Hey! Slow down!" I ordered.

He ignored what I said. He then aimed the limo toward the side of a building at the end of the street. As we got closer, he honked the horn to tell the people on the sidewalk to get out of the way. I quickly realized what was about to happen.

"Oh, crap."

I got as far into the back of the limo as I could and buckled the seat belt tightly. The people on the sidewalk ran for their lives, screaming. I clenched onto the seat belt and fabric on the seats as hard as I could.

The limo crashed into the building with a terrifyingly loud shock. In an instant, I was thrown forward and then slammed back into the seat. The shock of the crash sent an unbearable pain coursing through me, contorting my body, but luckily I was saved by my seatbelt. I stumbled out of the limo. I looked over and saw the chauffer's body out on top of the hood of the car covered with pieces of glass from the windshield. I struggled to my feet. I saw the people crowding around me on the sidewalk. Any one of them could spot me from a mile away. Everyone took out their phones and immediately took pictures of me.

"Look! It's Jack Miller!" "What's he doing here?" "Jack! When is your next album coming out!?" They all said as they blinded me with the flashes from their cameras.

I could barely comprehend what was happening. The memories kept playing in my head. I suddenly realized that myself, as a Perfect, this isn't who I really am.

I know now. My name isn't Jack Miller, its Hossan.. I broke out of the crowd of Perfects and stumbled into the road, where I saw a truck speeding towards me. My brain couldn't process what was happening. Everything from the truck heading toward me to the shock from the car crash was all a blur. But the memories, the memories all became clear to me. I didn't belong in Alpha city at all. I need to get back to Roderic, but how? The truck was still speeding towards me. It wasn't stopping, and there was no way that I could dodge it.

Just before the truck hit me, I remembered one more thing: Violeta and I talking while we were at the top of the hill in that park.

"I just don't want you to go."

That's what she said to me a long time ago. And what was it that I said to her?

"I'm always gonna be here for you."

That's right. I'm going to make sure of that. I'm going to make sure that she'll be perfectly fine. That as long as I can be by her side, nothing will ever be able to touch us.

The second after I remembered that, everything went black.

I opened my eyes and, strangely enough, I found myself inside a glass container full of water. Or at least I think its water. I wriggled my fingers around and it felt thick like slime. When I tried to open my eyes, a really bright light was flashing down on me. I almost thought I'd gone blind.

I turned away, looking way from the light. I felt incredibly weak, even more than before. I felt a clear mask covering my entire face. I quickly realized that it was feeding me the air I was breathing. I found long, clear tubes connecting to my body, some thin and some wide. The wider ones poked into my arms, legs, and chest through the holes in my suit. I got a closer look at the tubes and saw black fluid being pumped out.

I pulled off the mask and sat up with the tubes still connected in my body. Completely freaked out I quickly tried to pull some of the tubes out from my body. I started with the thin ones. A tremendous, stinging pain rattled my body as I removed the tubes. After taking out the last thin tube, I moved on to removing the wider ones. The second I grabbed one, I felt an intense pain coursing throughout my body. I squealed as I saw the tube pulling on my flesh as I pulled it out. I gave up, and tried to get out of the tub. I carefully made my way out of the container. I put my foot up over the glass container and slipped, falling to the ground. Whatever tubes I hadn't pulled out of myself were ripped out of my body by the force of the fall.

I pushed my body off of the floor and got onto my feet. My coordination was completely shot. I looked around the room and saw a horrifying sight. Dozens of other humans were hooked up to tubes in glass containers like mine. It was a grotesque sight. In disgust, I threw up all over the ground. Strangely enough, I was relieved at the sight of my own vomit. It was colored in a greenish red. It reminded me that I was a human again.

I looked around and found more humans in containers with fluids. My vision was still hazy so it was difficult to discern objects. Walking around, I bumped into something with my back. I turned around to see what it was. I saw what I thought was a human laying on top of a long metal table. I rubbed my eyes in order to make my vision clearer. I gasped in horror at what I saw.

It was one of the Perfects. A man. He wore a white robe, and his smile mask had been removed. His real face underneath was wrinkly and colored in a deep gray. Veins pushed against his clammy, raw face. Wide tubes connected to his arms, legs, and chest feeding him the black sludge. I followed the tubes back to my own container. As I put two and two together, horror followed disgust. The thought of the Perfects stealing the fluids from humans and putting them into their own bodies completely horrified me. I looked around the room at other people's containers. The wide tubes fed into tanks labeled *Formula H*, collecting the fluids.

Luckily, the Perfect seemed to be sleeping. I looked around and found his smile mask on a nearby table. The smile was still there as usual. The mask sat on top of a black uniform with gold trimmings on the edges. I figured it belonged to this guy. Then I spotted the Perfect's pistol. I reached my hand out to pick it up. I was shaking in my own skin as my hand got closer and closer to the pistol. I pulled myself back, rethinking the idea. I'd never even touched a gun before. I'd probably cause more harm than good with it.

My vision eventually cleared completely and I felt like I regained some of my strength. I saw a door at the end of the room. I stumbled through the door as it opened automatically. More humans were lined against the walls in containers. A long, wheeled table sat in the middle of the room. Harnesses hung from the sides of the table and a tray of surgical tools was placed in a shelf underneath. Suddenly, I heard voices coming through another door at the end of the room. If anyone found me, it would mean the end for me. I quickly hid behind one of the containers. A few seconds later two Perfects entered the room. They looked like scientists judging from their white robes, rubber gloves, and the surgical masks hanging from their necks.

"Alright, let's get started. I know you're a trainee and you're new to all of this, but I need you to do what I say," said one of the Perfects. I figured he was more experienced and was in charge of training him.

The trainee Perfect nodded and spoke, "I'm sorry but, which ones are being harvested and which ones are we doing the experiments on again?" the trainee asked.

"Are you serious? I've told you at least a million times already," the trainer said with a sigh. "Look, the tanks with blue tags are the ones being harvested and the ones with the green tags are being experimented on. Got it?" he asked. The trainee Perfect simply nodded.

Suddenly, a cell phone started to ring in the room. One of the Perfects pulled out his cell phone and answered the call.

"Hello? Oh, hey. Yeah, it's just me and the trainee in here. We're on our last shift now." There was a short pause. "I'm fine. I'm alright. How are you?" Another short pause. The trainee looked bored, shifting around on his feet.

"Okay, I'll see you later. Bye." He then turned off his phone and put it down next to one of the containers. "Let's just get this over with. I really wanna get outta here."

"Yeah. Let's get the tools," replied the trainee.

"Yeah. Go get one of them," the trainer said, pointing to the containers.

The trainee then walked over to one of the containers with a green tag on it. He carefully pulled out each of the tubes out of the man in the tub and turned off the machine to which it was connected.

He then picked up the person inside the container, a still unconscious man, and brought him over to the table. He slowly and very carefully laid out the unconscious man down on the table. The two of them then tightened harnesses to the human's arms and legs.

"When's he going to wake up?"

The trainee asked, handing the scalpel from the tray underneath to the trainer.

"Soon. Any second now," the trainer replied.

The man then slowly opened his eyes. He tried to move his arms, but he found them tied down. He then saw the two Perfect scientists, standing above him like skyscrapers.

"What's going on!? Where am I!?" he asked, obviously scared and surprised.

The two Perfects ignored his questions.

"Are we going to use any sedatives on this thing?" the trainee asked the other Perfect scientist.

"Nah, we want to get real reactions from each specimen. It'll provide better data for the rest."

"What are you going to do to me?" the man asked, now fearing the worst.

The trainer leaned in with the scalpel in his hand and pointed it at the man's stomach. I was sure the man knew what was about to happen.

"Wait, wait, wait! Hold on a second!" he said as he squirmed on the table.

It was no use. The Perfect dug the scalpel into the man's belly, and then moved it laterally across. The scalpel tore through the flesh. The man's blood started with small drops onto the floor, then poured over like a shower.

The man's agonizing screams were amplified with every new cut the trainer made. I couldn't believe the horror I was witnessing. I wanted to help that man, but I knew if I tried, I'd have no chance of escape. I saw that the Perfect's cell phone was still sitting next to one of the other containers. If I could get to it, I could take videos and pictures of all of the horrors in here.

I slowly sneaked over to the cell phone. Making as little noise as possibly, I quickly snatched it. I activated the camera and started taking video of what they were doing. As I recorded more footage, the man's screams only got louder. I felt nauseous watching. I could barely stand to listen, but I had no choice

Soon the man passed out from the pain. The two Perfects were fiddling around with the man's organs. One of them then pulled a strange device shaped like a small computer chip from his pocket and pushed it into the man's chest.

"Alright, let's see if it works," the trainer said as he activated the device.

A short beep indicated that the device was now turned on. The man's once motionless body began to fidget and spasm wildly on the table. Hope and excitement could be heard in the voices of the Perfects as they shouted out excitedly.

"C'mon!' Let's go!"

Soon, however, the man's body became motionless once again. About half a minute had passed. The human was surely dead by now, and the two Perfects looked annoyed.

"Dammit! It didn't work," the trainer yelled out of frustration. "Whatever..." he said as he faced the Perfect trainee. "Alright, we're done here. Dump the body," he said as he headed to the exit before throwing off his bloodied rubber gloves into a nearby trash can.

The trainee pushed the table holding the corpse out of the room. The wheels under the metal desk squeaked against the floor as it was pushed to the other side of the room. I followed him, continuing to capture every moment with the camera phone. I saw him push the table up to a small door in the wall. He opened the door, revealing a dark shaft. The trainee tilted and shook the table until the corpse fell in. I heard a faint crash at the bottom of a shaft. The trainee then closed the door and pushed the table away and out the exit.

Now alone, I went over to the chute where the trainee had dumped the corpse. I opened it and looked down the shaft. To my horror and surprise, I saw an enormous pile of corpses at the bottom of the chute. All of them were human bodies. I could taste and even feel the stench of rotting decay from the corpses. I felt like throwing up again, but I held it down.

Then I remembered trainer saying that they were doing experiments on the humans they had. What if *I* had some sort of strange device inside of me? I quickly ran back into the room and over to the container I was in earlier. There was a blue tag on my tank, which would mean that I was being harvested. Strangely, I was glad. I think I'd much rather be harvested than experimented on.

I took more video footage of the containers and the humans inside the containers. While taking footage, I noticed something. All of the people in the tanks were large, male humans. Then it hit me. I remembered reading in the newspaper about increased kidnappings in Roderic. What if these guys were the same men who I read about being kidnapped? This terrified me. I had to find a way out of this place. I went out into the hallway and walked around, trying to find an exit.

I silently crept through the hallways. I noticed that there were windows as large as garage doors. Bright light from the windows seeped into the darkness of the halls. I looked through one of the windows. The walls inside were all white in the small rooms. Nothing inside but blinding light from a single source on the ceiling. I walked over to the next room and saw the same exact thing. Inside the next room, however, I saw something that was even more horrifying and grotesque than the live surgery experiment done by the Perfects.

On the other side of the giant glass barrier separating me from what was inside the room was a horrific creature. An enormous creature, with pink, bloody skin, as if it had been turned inside out. All of its muscles were engorged. Its face looked distorted with the mouth, eyes, nose and ears in awkward positions, as if ripped across its face. All its veins were pushing up against the creature's skin. My first thought was that it was a freak accident of one of the experiments done by the Perfects. It laid on the floor looking weak and exhausted, and it was breathing very heavily.

I saw a numbered keypad beside the window. I'd let this poor creature out if I knew the code. I felt sorry for it. But then I thought, what if it attacks me? That thing looked like it could probably throw a truck as if it were a football. Next to the keypad, I saw there was a clipboard hanging on the wall with a paper attached to it. I grabbed it and read: *Test subject H355. Specimen 12 in body alteration experiment 226. Jurica Balgoy.* For some reason, the name Jurica Balgoy definitely rang a bell. While I was trying to remember, the creature lifted its head off of the ground and spotted me behind the glass barrier.

Its eyes widened and it glared at me ferociously. I felt like it was looking through me, as if it knew me. I was instantly frightened by its glaring visage. It stood up from the ground slowly. I felt the force of earthquakes coming from the room with each step the creature took. It extended its gargantuan arms out, as if stretching. It made tight fists. It was breathing heavier and heavier as it continued to glare at me. It was obviously angry, but why? Then, I saw it: a long scar stretching across the monster's right cheek. It was the same scar of the guy that mugged me on the train a long time ago. I realized exactly who this creature really was.

Of course he'd be mad at me. He must think that it's my fault, that I made him like this. He slowly got closer to the glass barrier. He raised his tight, car-sized fists high above his head and then brought them straight into the glass. The barrier vibrated with tremendous force from the smash of the monster. The glass still held together despite the blows. He smashed his fists onto the glass again. I felt the force travel through the floor as I lost my balance and fell to the ground. Again and again, he banged against the glass, the glass remaining completely solid. Suddenly, a small crack in the glass appeared. At that exact moment, an unbearably loud alarm screamed in the hallway and a bright red light blinked from the ceiling. I tried to cover my ears from the noise but it barely helped. Jurica also tried to cover his ears, but it didn't look like it was of any use to him either. He was writhing around on the ground, trying to block out the noise.

Somehow, through all of the noise, I heard voices coming from down the hallway.

"This way! Over here!"

I knew that it had to be the Perfects. They were coming from the lab. I ran down to the end of the hallway and turned the corner. I waited behind the corner to watch what was happening in the hallway. There were three men. One scientist and two giant Perfect men holding large batons. The scientist ran over to the keypad and typed in a code. The glass barrier lifted up and opened.

"Go!" the scientist commanded, pointing at Jurica.

The two large men then flipped switches on their batons. Instantly, electric shocks started to rush through the end of the sticks. One of the men raised his baton high above his head. Jurica was lying on the floor, trying to shield his ears from the sounds of the alarms. With great force, the baton came crashing down onto the monster's head, shocking him, and he shook as if lightning had struck him. One strike after another, the two men smashed down the batons onto Jurica's body, without any sign of mercy.

Several minutes passed and Jurica's body was becoming even more disfigured with each strike. I recorded everything with the camera phone. It was all I could do. From where I was down the hallway, I zoomed in on what was left of Jurica's face. He was cringing on the ground, and the look on his face showed that he couldn't take much more of this torture. I then focused the camera at the two giant Perfects. Their masks still showed the same smiles like the rest. They seemed to be enjoying what they were doing.

"Okay, that's enough. We don't want to kill the thing. We still need to run tests on this one."

One of the large Perfects put away his baton. The other Perfect smacked Jurica one last time before laughing. I was sure they enjoyed doing that. They shut the glass barrier and left.

"That was awesome!" one of the gargantuan Perfects said as he and the rest left the hall back through the labs.

Once they were gone, I went over to Jurica's room and looked through the glass. His battered body looked even worse than it had before. He laid on the floor in the same position he was in when I first found him. I felt sorry for him as I kept the cell phone camera rolling on him. With whatever strength Jurica had left in his body, he lifted up his head a few inches off the floor and looked at me with bloodshot eyes.

"I'll come back for you," I said as I quietly walked away.

Moving down the hallway I saw a light creeping from under a large metal door at the end of the hall. I walked closer towards the light. I put my hand on the door handle and opened it. Immediately, an intense brightness shined from the room, blinding me and filling the once dark hallway with light. When my vision finally cleared, I witnessed another horrifying sight. An enormous room with thousands of cages holding monsters identical to Jurica. All with bloody pink skin and distorted faces. Perfects walked around on top of catwalks high above my head. It was just one terrible sight after another. With my hand shaking, I raised the cell phone and took footage of the room.

How many people have been taken and turned into these things? Suddenly, a voice called out.

"Hey, you!"

It came from one of the Perfects on the catwalk. My cover was blown. Just before I ran, I saw that the Perfect ripped out a walkie-talkie. As I left, I heard what he yelled into his radio.

"Security! We've got a human escaping from the labs! I repeat, a human is escaping from the labs!"

In the hallways, I ran in any direction that seemed like it might take me to an exit.

"There it is! The human!" a voice called out.

Two large Perfects stood at the other end of the hall. They both drew their batons and flipped on the switches. I panicked, fearing that I would end up like Jurica and the other monsters here. I looked around for any immediate exit. The light from the other room revealed a door near my side. I quickly burst through it, taking me to a staircase. I figured that if I just went down as fast as I could, I could get to the ground, and from there it would be easier to find an exit out of the building.

"He's in the stairs!" one of the Perfects called into his walkie-talkie.

I rushed down the stairs as fast as I could. I heard a voice on the floor above me.

"There!" one of the Perfects called out.

Two more of the Perfects rushed down the stairs, chasing me. I ran down as fast as I could. The sounds of the Perfect's boots hitting the cold metal stairs echoed through the stairway. I had no idea where I was going. I just figured the exit would be on the ground floor.

I found myself in the ground floor of the stairwell. There was a door at the bottom of the stairs. I blew through it quickly, revealing myself to a crowd of Perfects mostly standing around in the lobby of the building. They all wore normal suits so I didn't take them for security. I knew there was no time. I rushed into the crowd at full speed. Stiff-arming my way through, causing some people to fall.

"C'mon! Catch it!" I heard a security guard yell from across the room. I saw my ticket out, the front doors.

I rushed through the doors. It was a cold, rainy night. I was still wearing the same white suit that the Perfect gave me when I first brought in my lottery ticket. I was barefoot, and I was drenched from the fluids of the container and the rain. Feeling the rain on my face felt so refreshing. The Perfects walking by glanced at my odd appearance but didn't really care. I slipped into the crowd of Perfects walking by. I shivered in the cold as I tried to make my way through the crowds. I could hear the security guards still trying to find me.

"Find that human!" "C'mon! Where is it!?" they yelled as they looked through the crowds. The guards were flashing flash lights into the faces of everyone they saw. I tried to stay as far away from them as possible.

Giant screens on the sides of buildings lit up most of the streets. As usual, the TV shows and advertisements. But then they changed. All of screens changed all at the same time. I couldn't believe what I seeing. It showed a live broadcast of the Mayor.

"Attention, all citizens! This is your Mayor, Michael Rollins."

Everyone stopped to look up at the screens that towered over and around the city. A picture of my face appeared on the screens.

"This human is named Hossan. He is extremely dangerous! He has recently killed ten Perfects! A large reward will be given to whomever finds Hossan, dead or alive! And if a human finds him, not only will they receive the money, but they will also be able to be transformed into a Perfect! The body must be provided as evidence! Bring the body to the Alpha city government building! Thank you very much!"

That announcement played on every screen in Alpha. The same message must've been broadcast to the people in Roderic as well. The message caught the attention of everyone around me. The Perfects and the humans. This was not good. The Perfects would want to find me because they think that I killed some of the Perfects, and the humans would want to find me just for the reward.

The message played again and again, still showing my picture on the giant screens. These screens were so massive that anyone looking out their window in Roderic would clearly see my face. While everyone was staring at the screens, I ran away as fast as I could, covering my face with my hands. I needed help. I needed some sort of edge over the Perfects. Of course I already did have something. I still had the cell phone with all of the video footage of everything in the labs. But I needed help getting out of the city. Help from someone that I knew or at least thought could help me.

I ran around, thinking about all of the people who might be able to help me. Lidiya? No way, she'd wouldn't even waste her breath talking with me. Violeta? No, she doesn't come to Alpha city. Besides, she probably hates me. Then it hit me. Bartek. Bartek could definitely help me. He could be my cover to try to get back into Roderic and I'd be home free.

I recognized the streets and I knew exactly how I could get to the building where Bartek worked. After running through crowds of people I recognized the building. I ran over to get closer and that's when I saw him. From the other side of the street, I saw Bartek just past the glass doors. He was mopping the floors, as usual. I could see that he had headphones in his ears. He might have not yet heard of the reward or that I'd escaped. I was relieved that I might finally be able to get some help from someone.

M eanwhile, the lab's security officials met with Mayor Michael Rollins at his office at the top level of the Alpha city government building, the tallest building in Alpha. The Mayor sat behind a glass desk at the end of the circular room. Behind his desk were giant, floor-to-ceiling glass windows, providing a proper view of all of Alpha city.

The three Perfects that met Mayor Rollins were the lab's chief security officials. They stood like towers beside each other – enormous men with deep, fear-inducing voices and arms strong enough to rip apart trucks. Nervous sweat trickled down their necks as they stood like statues in front of Mayor Rollins. Just the mere sight of this man scared the three Perfects half to death. The Mayor stuck a long cigar in his mouth. He slowly snatched a lighter from the top of his desk, next to an ash tray full of butts and a mountain of ash. He lit the tip and breathed in. The glow of the heat consumed more of the cigar as Michael Rollins drew in deep breaths. He then looked up at the three men.

"So... describe to me exactly what happened," he said, sounding obviously unhappy and dissatisfied as he puffed out a cloud of smoke.

The man standing to the far left of Mayor Rollins spoke.

"S-sir, we did all that we could. The human escaped before we could get enough men on top of him."

The man pathetically tried to explain. Mayor Rollins did nothing more than puff out another cloud of smoke. Each of them was growing more and more nervous as the air in the room became heavier.

"Uh... uh, we also believe he took footage of the lab. Security camera footage shows this."

The Perfect motioned to the man to his side who was holding onto a picture. He walked over to Mayor Rollins's desk and dropped the picture in front of the Mayor. It showed a picture of Hossan holding up the phone to record Jurica from the other side of the glass barrier. Mayor Rollins glared at the picture and said nothing.

"Do we have a file on this guy?" the Mayor asked.

"Yes, we do," the man answered.

He then handed the Mayor a file. Mayor Rollins slowly opened it. The file held a picture of Hossan, as well as his personal information. The Mayor stood up from his desk and picked up the file.

One of the other men started to speak.

"Sir, we've also put out rewards for this man's capture or killing. We're sure that he will be taken down soon," he said.

"Oh yeah? And what about the phone?" the Mayor replied, puffing out more smoke as about half of the cigar now turned to ash.

The three of them cringed at Mayor Rollins's reply.

"We need that phone. I don't care about killing this guy as much as getting the phone. The phone is what's important. Also..."

"Also?" The men asked.

The Mayor then took the file and angrily threw it right into the Perfect's faces. The file hit one of the men in his face while the rest of the papers fluttered all around them.

"How the hell did a human get past our security system, huh!? I mean, what the hell am I paying you idiots for!?" the Mayor yelled out.

"So... what are you going to do?" One of the men asked.

The Mayor walked up to him, and spoke, seething with anger.

"Excuse me? Is that a fucking question? It's none of your goddamn business what I'm going to do next," the Mayor said angrily as he blew out a cloud of smoke into the man's face. "You got a fucking problem with that?" the Mayor finished. The security man coughed out and tried to clear his throat from all of the smoke.

"No, sir," he pathetically said as he coughed some more.

The Mayor then walked over to his desk and shoved the cigar into his ashtray.

"Alright... you know what I'm going to do now?" the Mayor said.

He didn't wait for any answers and spoke.

"What I'm going to do is I'm going to start tying up loose ends," he said.

"Loose ends, sir?" one of the men asked.

The Mayor then pulled open one of the drawers in his desk, revealing a fully loaded pistol. He looked down at the pistol, but didn't show any of the men the gun.

"Hey..," the Mayor started. "Any of you guys have family? Like kids or a wife or whatever," he said calmly.

All of the men nodded.

"Yeah, we do," one of them said.

"Good. Think about 'em," the Mayor said as he pulled out, and cocked back the pistol.

"Because it's the last thing any of you think about." Mayor Rollins then shot the pistol.

The Mayor shot three bullets, BANG BANG BANG, right into the man on his far left. He hit the floor with a hard thud.

"Oh crap!" one of the others screamed, and ran for the door. The Mayor didn't hesitate to put two rounds right into his back.

One man was left. He stood alone, paralyzed in fear. He shook in his boots while watching his friend's fluids flow out of his body. He then felt something against his head. The man turned around, and saw the pistol pressed up against his forehead. And in an instant, BANG.

I made it just feet from the door.

"Hey! There's the human!" someone in front of me yelled.

My hands were pulled away from my face by a Perfect. He held my hands together in his grip and called out.

"Over here! Over here!" he yelled to the security guards.

I knew I couldn't go back there, back to the labs. I pulled one of my arms free from the Perfect's grip. I brought my arm back, and punched the Perfect right in his face. He screamed out and covered his face, cursing and yelling. The moment I broke free, even more Perfects tried to grab me. I tried to wrestle away from them all as I bolted through the mass of Perfects walking around. I reached the edge of the sidewalk and ran onto the street. I made a break for it. My fear fueled me to I hurry through two lanes of traffic, very nearly getting hit by a truck, again.

I made it to the other side of the street and turned the corner into a back alleyway between two buildings. I turned around and saw that I'd lost them. Thinking I was safe, I breathed a sigh of relief before seeing something turn the corner at the other end of the alleyway. It was a giant solid metal robot with massive legs supporting its body. Arms equally as massive stretched out from its sides. It had a cone-shaped head on top of its body and the word POLICE written boldly across its midsection. I could see a camera in its cone head was swiveling around, and soon it stopped to look straight at me. It was as if it knew exactly who I was. Then, holes on the top of the robot's shoulders opened up. They revealed small cones that flashed out red and blue lights as a siren was blasted out at full volume. It was like a giant walking police car.

I tried to run back to the other side of the alleyway but there was another one of the robots. It had its lights flashing and its siren on. I was trapped, and with no way out, I had no idea what to do. The rain poured harder on top of my head, and it didn't help me as I frantically tried to find some sort of escape.

Both of the robots started to move closer to me, their tank treads speeding quickly towards me. I was going to be crushed under them. I was panicking without a clue of what to do. Then, out of some sort of super-human impulse, I ran towards the first robot. I lowered myself down, sliding under and through the legs of the robot. I couldn't believe what I just did. It was like something straight out of an action movie. Once I was behind the police robot I turned to look at it. Its camera swiveled back to look at me as if saying in awe, "Dude, what did you just do?"

Then the camera turned back to its front. The robot was still speeding ahead and smashed right into the other robot. They both crashed and collapsed to the ground, followed by a loud explosion and a blaze igniting from the wreck. Their lights and sirens shut off as they burned to a crisp.

I knew I didn't have any time to sit still. I couldn't see them, but I could hear the voices of the Perfects from the other side of the burning wreck. It sounded like they were freaking out back there.

"Oh my God!" "What's happening!?" they all screamed.

I ran out of the alleyway and quickly made my way to the building that Bartek worked in. I pushed open the glass doors and found Bartek mopping the floors in his regular janitor uniform. His back was turned away from me as he was listening to music through his headphones. When I got close enough, I grabbed onto his shoulder and turned him around. His eyes widened and the mop dropped from his hands and hit the floor. It was as if he'd seen a ghost. Bartek pulled the headphones off and spoke.

"H-Hossan... what are you... how are you here? I thought you were turned into one of the Perfects! What happened!?" I tried to reply, but I couldn't catch my own breath from all of the running.

"Look, there's no time to explain. I need to borrow your regular clothes. We've got to get outta here!" I explained, still out of breath.

Bartek didn't hesitate. We quickly went into the locker room. Bartek turned open his locker.

"Wanna tell me why do you need my clothes?" Bartek asked.

"I found out something big about the Perfects. They've been killing and using the humans in labs," I explained as I started changing.

"Oh yeah? Using them for what?" Bartek asked, confused.

"I don't know. But they definitely want me dead, and they've even put out a reward for me."

"What kind of reward?" Bartek asked.

I feared if I told him what the reward was, he'd try to turn me in.

"It's nothing. It's not important."

I finished changing. I looked like any other human in Bartek's clothes. I topped off the outfit with a baseball cap that someone had left in the locker room. I pulled the front of the hat over my face.

"Alright, let's go," I said to Bartek.

We approached a group of Perfects as we made our way to the exit. We passed by them as they were looking at news about me on their phones. They were talking about the reward and observing my face on their phones.

"Does anybody know where this guy is?" "Man, I so want that money," they all said to each other.

It didn't seem like they recognized my face. I guessed I was pretty much in the clear with Bartek's clothes on. No Perfect would ever bother to look at a normal human's face. And with Bartek's clothes, I looked like any other normal human.

"Where are we going?" Bartek asked.

I responded, frustrated with everything that's been happening. "We're going to the train station. We've got to get outta Alpha city, and back to Roderic."

"You know, you still haven't explained fully to me what happened," he said.

"I'll explain later. Let's just focus on getting to the trains as fast as we can, alright?" I replied as we neared the train station.

Bartek and I climbed to the platform above as the train arrived.

"Come on, let's go!" I yelled as I pulled Bartek quickly into the train.

We got in, and thankfully, there were only few people besides us in the train. We took our seats next to each other on the benches.

"Okay, *now* do you wanna tell me what's happening? Wanna explain to me what's going on?" Bartek said, sounding obviously annoyed.

I pulled out the camera phone and played the video footage I took.

"Look," I said as I handed Bartek the phone.

A few seconds passed with Bartek watching the video.

"What is this?" he asked, confused.

"Just watch," I told him.

Bartek went back to watching the video. It got to the part with the live surgery. Bartek's eyes focused on the video.

"What the..,"

His eyes widened in horror and disgust, and his mouth gaped open. Bartek tried to form words to comment on the video, but watching the video made it impossible for him to articulate his thoughts into words.

The video ended, and Bartek saw everything. It took him a little bit for Bartek to digest what he had just watched. After swallowing the feeling of his disgust, Bartek was able to speak.

"Was that real?" He asked.

"Yeah."

"What was it? What were they doing?"

"It's all of the footage I could get of the inside of some sort of lab in Alpha city. It's all run by the Perfects. They're harvesting and experimenting on the humans."

"How could they do this? Why would they do this?" Bartek asked.

He then handed the phone back to me. I noticed that his hand was shaking as he passed it over to me. I turned off the phone and put it back into my pocket.

"I don't know. But I'd really like to find out," I said as I looked out the window. The lights of Alpha city shined brightly through the night sky as we got further and further away.

"I'm sure we can get answers from the Mayor of Alpha city," I said with an attitude of confidence. I want revenge for everything that the Perfects have done. I'm making that as clear as possible.

"There's no way you're going to even be able to get close to Mayor Rollins," Bartek replied.

"Yeah, but if we show this video to everyone, everyone'll probably get real angry. Angry enough to start a revolution. Think about it, the humans versus the Perfects in total war."

"I don't think that's going to work."

"They may have better technology than us but we have numbers. Don't you see? We can win!" I said enthusiastically as I clapped my hands together.

Bartek thought about it for a little while before making up his mind.

"You know what? I think it'll work," Bartek said. I nodded my head, agreeing with him.

"But before we do anything, I've got to take care of something," I said.

Just before the train arrived in the station, I asked Bartek a question.

"Bartek. How come you believe everything I'm saying? I mean, it doesn't sound ridiculous to you at all?" Bartek looked at me, then replied.

"Well, yeah, it does sound ridiculous. But you being alive and back to being a human is even more incredible than what is on that phone."

When the train stopped at the station in Roderic, Bartek and I quickly stepped out onto the platform. I said one last thing to Bartek just before we separated.

"Wait for me in the park! I've gotta take care of something. I'll meet you there in twenty minutes!"

maneuvered through crowds of people, trying not to waste any time. I didn't wait for people to get out of my way. I pushed them out of the way. I was only focused on one thing right now. I knew exactly what I needed to do.

I went to the old apartment where I used to live. I figured Violeta had to be there. I pushed on the call box next to the main door and called my room.

"Violeta! Violeta I'm back! Let me in, please!" I screamed.

It was no use. I got impatient. I stepped back and I drove my foot into the old wooden door. The door burst open on my first try. I ran up the stairs as fast as I could.

"Violeta! Violeta I'm here!" I yelled as I climbed up the stairs.

I reached my room and saw the door wide open. As I got closer, I noticed a putrid odor coming from the room. I stepped inside to see the room in a horrible mess.

"Violeta?" I said, trying to cover my nose from the smell.

I called out her name again. The light from the TV revealed Violeta sleeping on the bed. I walked over to her and tried to wake her. I shook her, trying to roll her over. When she finally moved, a syringe dropped out of her hand and rolled out onto the floor. I stopped trying to wake up Violeta and picked up the syringe. I saw black gunk stuck to the inside of the syringe and looked over to see small bloodied holes on Violeta's forearm. It quickly became clear to me exactly what Violeta had been doing while I was gone.

I threw away the syringe and went back to Violeta. I shook her body harder this time, even screaming out her name. It was no use. I went over to a shelf above the kitchen counter to take out a glass and filled it with water. I walked over to Violeta with the glass of water in my hand. I figured that she'd probably hate me for doing this, but I had to do it.

I splashed the water into Violeta's face. She immediately woke up in a frenzy.

"What!? What's happening!?" she screamed as she flailed around in the bed.

"Violeta! Calm down!" I yelled as I grabbed hold of her shoulders and turned her to face me.

She was just as, if not even more surprised than Bartek. Her eyes didn't come off my face when she saw me.

"It's not possible. How are you... here?" she said, as she put her hand on my face.

Our eyes met as the moonlight crept in, illuminating the room. It felt magical.

I was ready to kiss her, but in a split second she slapped me across the face. I tumbled out of the bed and onto the ground. I put my own hand on my cheek and felt my face sting. I didn't say anything, I was too startled. After leaving her all alone and abandoning her the way I did, I definitely deserved it.

"What are you doing here?" she asked, still sitting on the bed.

"I came back to be with you. I missed you a lot," I replied.

"If you missed me then why didn't you come back to me earlier? Besides how are you a human? I thought you were transformed into one of the Perfects," she said.

"Yeah. I can explain." I pulled out the cell phone from my pocket.

"This phone has some information about the Perfects. You've got to see it! It's going to bring them down for good!" I tried to motion the phone towards Violeta so that she could see what was on it but she stopped me. Her arm stretched out to block me away.

"I don't want to see anything you have! You left me all alone! What makes you think I want anything to do with you!?"

I moved back to make space and put the phone away.

"I know. It's my fault, it's all my fault! I didn't know what I was doing. I came back because I missed you. I knew that I didn't belong there, with them. I belong here with you. I want to be everywhere you are. I want to be by your side no matter what."

"Why? Why do you want to be with me so badly?" Violeta asked.

"Because, I love you."

Violeta's eyes widened. She was speechless. I thought I was done for, I'd lost her. Suddenly, I heard something that sounded like whimpering. I looked up and saw tears falling from Violeta's face. I immediately felt worried for her.

"Are you okay?" I asked, as I got closer.

"That's it," she said.

Violeta lifted her head up, revealing the tears from her deep blue eyes and the sound of her crying mixed in with her voice.

"That's all I ever wanted to hear from you," she said with tears raining down her cheeks and a wide, beautiful smile across her face. I didn't want to see Violeta cry at all.

"I hope you're just crying because you're happy," I said. I quickly leaned in and hugged Violeta. I could feel her heartbeat up against my own, and the warmth of our bodies.

"Thanks for coming back," Violeta replied, with her face buried in my chest and arms.

I lifted her chin up to be level with mine. My face was only about an inch or two away from hers. I stared into her deep, blue eyes. It was like looking at the universe through a window. I then leaned in slowly and softly kissed her lips. I pressed down gently, trying my best not to be too rough. As it all happened, little sparks of happiness set off across my body. It made my skin tingle and it felt great. Our eyes met again, staring into each other's souls. And almost instinctively, we kissed again and again. My lips started to hurt a bit. I pushed back to signal a stop to the kissing. Violeta was smiling greatly, and her blush cast a deep red across her face. It was a dream come true for me.

Violeta looked down at my pocket and pointed to it.

"So what's on your cell phone?" she asked. I had almost forgotten about the video, I was so enthralled in kissing Violeta.

"Oh, oh right," I said as I pulled the phone out from my pocket and turned it on.

I brought Violeta up to the bed. She sat next to me so that we could watch it together, although I didn't want to watch it at all. I played the video and Violeta watched.

Violeta watched until it got to the middle of the live surgery. Suddenly, Violeta stopped the video and turned off the cell phone. She quickly passed the phone over to me. She stared at the ground with a blank expression on her face. It made me miss the expression she had on her just a while ago when we were kissing. Suddenly, Violeta spoke softly.

"How... how could they do that to someone?" she asked.

I looked down at the floor and wondered with her, why?

"I have no idea. But we have to stop them. That's for sure!" I said proudly. Violeta nodded her head.

"So, what now?" Violeta asked as she stood up. I stood up as well and spoke.

"I know what to do. Get ready, we're going to the park. A friend of mine is going to meet us there."

Violeta quickly threw on a jacket and ran with me out of the apartment and over to the park. As we got closer to the park, we witnessed a small crowd of people gathering. The crowd was small, probably because most people would think that Bartek is just a crazy guy.

People were calling out, "What's going on!?" "Why'd you call us here!?"

I looked around for Bartek, when out of nowhere I heard someone calling out my name. Violeta and I looked around for the source of the sound. I spotted Bartek calling for me near the entrance of the park.

He was waving around both of his arms, yelling, "Hey! Over here!"

Violeta and I saw Bartek and we headed toward him. I grabbed onto Violeta's hand and we pushed through the crowds. I could feel her fingers laced around mine as I pushed more people out of the way.

I got in front of the crowds so that everyone around could see me, and I swear, I wanted to shout louder than all of the voices in world combined. Not out of anger, but out of a sense of urgency to get my message to people.

"My name is Hossan and I have something I need to tell everyone!" At first, only a few people were looking my way, but when they recognized my face, they immediately gasped. I knew beforehand that they wouldn't think I'm crazy since they must all recognize me as a winner of the Lucky Day lottery. Someone who once walked amongst the Perfects.

"Everything the Perfects told you all before are lies! As one of the Perfects, I couldn't remember my life as a human. I couldn't picture the faces of my friends! I managed to escape from Alpha city... with this!" I said, holding the cell phone high up.

"On this, I have footage of the Perfects harvesting humans and experimenting on them! I can give you my number, and you'll send me your numbers so that you too can see what I saw!" I proclaimed to the small crowd gathering before me.

"Hey! We wanna join, too!"

Dritan stood with his gang with a menacing smile, wearing the same leather jacket and dark clothes as before. I felt anger rise up inside of me the moment I saw him, but I held myself back. As much as I wanted to kill Dritan, I'd much rather face up against Mayor Rollins.

"What do you want?" I asked, angry to see him.

"Oh come on, I just wanna help. Can't we all just get along?" Dritan said sarcastically with the same unnatural smile.

As he and his gang walked toward me, people in the crowd stepped back away from Dritan and the Devilmen. Everyone knew who they were, and everyone feared for their lives around them.

"You destroyed Violeta's apartment and tried to kill us. Why would we even want to be around you?" I said. Dritan stepped closer as he spoke.

"Listen, I'm sorry about that, and I wish I could take it back. But you're not gonna go anywhere unless you let the Devilmen get your back."

"Why's that?" I asked in confusion.

"Because you don't have any good weapons. We've got all the guns and bombs you could ever need. You'll have a better chance with us around, trust me."

I thought about it for a little bit. Dritan was probably right. I'm not going to be able to do anything without their weapons and man power.

"Okay, fine. But why do you want to help us so badly?"

Dritan's smile disappeared, and he spoke with absolute seriousness. "I saw the video you took. It really got to me, as it got to everybody here. The Perfects don't mean anything to us now," he declared. "I already told my guys to set everything up for the big fight. We're all meeting up at the headquarters. So c'mon let's go," Dritan said as he motioned me to follow him. Just before Violeta and I left with Dritan to their headquarters, I spoke my last words to the crowd in front of me.

"Everyone! Make sure you spread the video to everyone you know! We need to make sure that every single human sees this!" I yelled confidently before giving my number to one person and sending them the video to let it be shared amongst everyone.

Violeta and I found ourselves following the Devilmen into a part of Roderic that was long forgotten, a godforsaken land where the sun never shines. A place where all forms of crime and pure evil thrive and come to get high. Violeta and I followed Dritan and his gang to a run down, old building that was like so many others in Roderic. Dritan knocked on the front door. An enormous man with a scar on his bald head opened the door. He took one look at Dritan and got out of his way. Dritan walked in with the other gang members. When I got close to the door, the enormous man stood in the doorway, blocking me from going inside.

"Woah! What do you think you're doing!?" He tried to grab at my shirt collar with his colossal hands. But just before he touched me, Dritan spoke.

"It's cool! Those guys are with us!" The enormous man got out of the way for us on Dritan's orders.

As soon as I walked in, I noticed a fowl stench in the air. I looked back over my shoulder and saw Violeta covering her nose and mouth. There was only a flickering light bulb in the middle of the hall as we walked in, and the floor boards creaked as we stepped on them. I turned to look inside of one of the rooms where I saw a few guys were playing cards.

"So this is your headquarters? It looks like crap," I commented.

"Yeah, that's what everyone says when they first come in here. Or they're at least thinking it," Dritan responded.

Dritan stopped at a door in the hallway. The door looked just about the same as every other part of the building, disgusting and old. Dritan opened the door revealing the stairs that led down into the basement. I could hear sounds coming from the bottom of the stairs.

"Right this way," Dritan said as he pointed into the stairwell.

Violeta and I slowly started walking down the stairs. I was hoping this wasn't going to be some sort of trap. Only Dritan followed us down, the rest of the other Devilmen that came with us walked away. As we walked down the stairs into the basement, we heard the sounds of fingers tapping on keyboards.

When we got all the way down stairs, Violeta and I saw about thirty people inside the basement. It was much larger than I thought it would've been. It was also much cleaner in the basement, the putrid smell from the first floor didn't exist down here. Most of the people down here had their faces glued to the screens of computers. There were at least twenty computers in this room, each with a tired, skinny man before it. I wasn't sure what they were doing on the computers, but I could see black windows with lines of numbers and letters scrolling down the screen. It reminded me of what I saw Erhan do on his computer when I last visited him.

On the other side of the room, I saw different people working over a large table and wearing medical masks. They were working with strange plants and white and brown powders.

"Hey what are they working on over there?" I asked Dritan, pointing over to the people with medical masks.

"They're making heroin. We have the largest heroin operation in all of Roderic." He walked over to a wooden crate, and reached his arms inside.

"If anyone ever tries to fuck with us we get at 'em with one of *these!*" Dritan said as he held up a giant machine gun. Dritan had a wild smile on his face as the sound of him cocking back the gun powerfully echoed through the entire room.

Dritan then looked over to the people working with the heroin. He saw one of them drop a little bit of the heroin on the floor, almost instantaneously, Dritan's smile disappeared and his eyes became fixed on the heroin makers.

"Hey, you!" Dritan shouted, pointing. "Be careful with that smack! I don't wanna have to go through the trouble of hiring new help because you dumbasses can't do your jobs!" he screamed.

The heroin workers quickly nodded their heads and went back to work. I felt uncomfortable being around Dritan, especially when he was angry and had a giant rifle in his hands.

I looked back over my shoulder to see how Violeta was doing. She was staring right at all of the heroin. She looked uneasy, as if she was holding herself back. Like a hungry tiger about to pounce on its prey. I tapped on her shoulder to get her attention.

"Hey, are you okay?" She turned to me with her eyes wide open.

"Uh, yeah. Yeah, I'm alright," she responded.

"Hey! Over here, you two!" Dritan called out.

He led us over behind an obese man with messy hair. He had his back turned to us while he stared at random papers stuck with magnets to a white board.

"Anton!" Dritan called out. The man didn't respond, his face practically glued to the papers.

"Anton!" He called out again.

The large man turned around to reveal himself. He was a large, pudgy man with thin fuzz covering his upper lip. He looked like the kind of person that would consider this basement his natural environment.

"Hello. My name's Anton," he said, sounding almost robotic.

He then offered his hand to me and Violeta. He shook Violeta's hand first. Immediately after she shook his hand, she wiped her hands on her pants. I found out why when I shook Anton's hand and noticed that he was sweating profusely.

"So they're the ones who shot the video and everything?"

"Yup," Dritan replied then immediately spoke out. "No actually, it's just the guy who shot the video. The girl is his girlfriend," Dritan said, pointing at us.

"Great. I'll take them now," Anton said.

"Yeah, yeah alright..," Dritan said as he went back to ogling the rifle.

Anton then turned to us, drawing in a deep breath through his mouth and spoke.

"So, have either of you got a plan for what you want to do?" he asked us. We both shook our heads and Anton sighed in response.

"Whatever, I'll just think of something," he responded. "I always do anyway," Anton said under his breath.

Dritan was too obsessed over the giant rifle and the drugs around him to hear what Anton said. However, I was able to hear him clearly.

Someone from the computers walked up to Anton and handed him a piece of paper.

"Oh, thank you," he said as he attached the paper to the white board with more magnets. I could clearly see it was a map of Alpha city.

Violeta and I stood behind Anton as he went over the papers on the board. He looked as immersed as anyone could be, but looking at it myself it was trying to look at a complicated puzzle. Not knowing where to start looking or analyzing.

Dritan put down the rifle and turned to face Anton's back.

"So, my man, have you figured out a plan?" He casually asked.

"No, not yet." Anton replied.

"C'mon I wanna shoot some people! Let's go!"

"Okay, okay. My brain's not a super computer," Anton said, going back to look at the papers when suddenly his eyes widened.

"Wait…" Anton said, slowly backing up from the board. "This just might work," he said with a wicked laugh as he turned to face us.

"Okay, this is the best way I see of us attacking Alpha city," he said, sounding very excited.

He then circled a spot on the Alpha city map with a marker right in the middle of the city.

"Right here is where the Alpha city government building is. That's where you'll find Mayor Rollins," Anton said, pointing at the spot.

"First, we've got to strike after the curfew. If we attack before then, they'll definitely see us coming. We'll be facing fire from riot police and their drones. And maybe even the military," Anton explained. I then remembered the robots I fought with in the alleyway when Anton mentioned drones.

"Hey, Police drones are the things with the cone-shaped heads and sirens on their shoulders, right?" I asked.

"Yeah. Why, have you ever seen one of them?" Anton asked. I nodded in response.

"Well they might look big and strong, but they're actually pretty weak," Anton said as he handed a piece of paper showing blueprints of a police drone.

"Their armor isn't bullet proof and they're actually pretty sensitive to fire," Anton pointed to the cone-shaped head on the police drone.

"All we have to do is smash this part." Anton said, pointing to the cone head. "Once we do that, it won't be able to see or complete any of its basic functions. After that, the drone will just slow down and it'll make it much easier to destroy them. Overheating them with fire would have the same effect as well." Anton turned back at the white board and the papers.

"Taking care of the riot police isn't going to slow us down too much unless they start using live rounds. If we cut enough of them down with guns and whatever else we have, we should be able to get past them before they can regroup in time. By the time they can actually get a hold on us, we'll already be covering a big chunk of the city."

Anton pushed another piece of paper into my arms. It was a picture of some sort of strangely shaped device with wires wrapped all around it.

"Those are the designs of the bombs we're going to use to make our entrance," Anton said as he pulled a marker from his pocket to circle three spots on the map.

"These are the tallest buildings in Alpha city besides the government building. If we blow a bunch of bombs at the main support columns at the very bottom of the buildings, it'll cause the towers to topple over. We don't have to destroy all of the supports, just a few will be enough.

"And that's our cue to attack?" I asked.

"Yes. My idea is we could use the bombings as a diversion. Then do a sneak attack from behind while there's another huge attack from the people at the Big Gate. Like a big, two-hit knockout!" Anton said as he pointed at the map. "And you and your girlfriend and maybe Dritan and some of his guys can protect you two while you make your way to the government building. You could ride motorcycles across the elevated train tracks into the city. It'll take much longer to get there, but it will probably a lot safer for you than anything else. All that matters is that you get to the government building. Once you get inside, you can do whatever you want with Mayor Rollins," Anton explained.

"How much time would all of this take?" I asked.

"As long as nothing happens, you could get there on motorcycles in about twenty minutes. In order to keep the police and military attention on the main rioters, we need them to create chaos for as long as possible. We're going to need some motorcycles, though, and that might be a problem," Anton explained. Then, an idea came to my head.

"Hey, I know a guy! His name is Hendri, he sells motorcycles. I think we can get them from him," I said.

"Good. Then we'll go with that. We create a diversion, and quickly make our way to the government building from the other side. Everyone all right with this?" Anton asked to us.

Dritan, Violeta, and I all nodded our heads.

"Good. All we need is the bikes and set up for the diversion attack. We're going to give out weapons to anyone who wants to join. That means we'll need the effort from a lot civvies to help us out."

At that moment, I remembered something important.

"Hey," I said, to get Anton's attention, "when I woke up and came out of a lab, inside they were doing experiments on humans.

I saw them. They're supposed to be super strong. We might be able to get help from them, too. If you saw the video then you'll know what I'm talking about."

"Yeah, the video is being shared around online so we all got to see it. We'll get them out. I just hope they don't go crazy." He said, with his arms casually out to everyone around him.

"Okay, let me summarize. First, we give out guns to everyone, then we plant the bombs, get everyone at the Big Gate, we blow the bombs, ride in, free those people from the labs, and finally kill the mayor."

"Got it," I acknowledged. I turned my head to look over to all of the guys at their computers. "What are they doing?" I asked Anton.

"Oh, they're exposing Alpha city's secrets. Hacking into government servers and databases. We're pulling everything about the kidnappings, how they control us, the experiments, everything and are putting it all up on the web. It was all my idea," Anton explained, sounding proud of himself. "They used to steal people's credit cards, now they steal secrets."

I got a closer look at one of the computer guys and recognized one of them.

"Erhan!" I yelled out. Erhan immediately popped up his head from the screen and when seeing me, we waved to each other.

"So whatever you do, don't do anything crazy. We need you to be ready for tomorrow," Anton advised.

"Oh, one more thing..," Dritan said as he walked over to a box sitting on top of a table. He pulled out two rectangular devices with antennae.

"Here, you'll both need these," he said as he handed me and Violeta the devices.

"They're walkie-talkies. We'll be able to talk to each other when the shit hits the fan. But in the meantime, get some rest. We'll call you up tomorrow to set up the bombs and try to organize our plan for attack. We'll send out a message to all of the people about it. So just go home and get some rest for now." Violeta and I nodded our heads and walked over to the staircase. I turned around once more to Dritan and Anton before I went up the stairs.

"Thanks!" I said.

"No, thank you!" Dritan said with a smile unlike his usual unnaturally wide smile. It was a nice, normal smile.

Violeta and I made our way back to the apartment. It was late and we were both pretty tired.

"I don't know about you, but I'm ready to go to bed," I said as I opened the door and walked into my room.

I laid the walkie-talkie down on the counter top. I stood in front of the bed as I spoke. "We should probably get to bed soon if we wanna-" I was interrupted by Violeta when she pushed me down onto the bed.

"Violeta?" I asked, laying on the bed and feeling confused.

Violeta sat down next to me on the bed. "What are you-" Violeta interrupted me again.

"Just shut up already," she said softly.

Violeta then spread her leg over my body and leaned in to kiss me. She raised her body over me with her knees to my sides. Violeta then leaned away, and slowly lifted her shirt up over her head to reveal her breasts. We were speechless, and the only sounds audible were short heavy breaths.

The next morning, I woke up with Violeta next to me. I laid on my side facing out to the window, watching the light of the sunrise pour into the room. Violeta laid beside me in darkness while I was soaked in the sunlight. Her arm stretched around my waist. I sat up to get out of the bed and stretch out. Noticing Violeta's arm still hanging on my waist, I slowly and carefully pushed it under the blanket. I got out of the bed to put my clothes on. Once I finished getting dressed, I looked back at Violeta still sleeping. Her hair was a mess, and with her still face, she looked angelic. The sunlight slowly washed over her face and Violeta began to wake up.

"Hey, Hossan. When did you wake up?" Violeta asked as she wiped her eyes with her hands.

"Not too long ago," I responded as I leaned back against the countertop. I noticed that there was drool on Violeta's face.

"You've got some stuff on your face," I said. Violeta wiped her face off in one sluggish swipe. At that point, the sunlight had fully lit the room. Suddenly, I heard a beeping noise in the room. It was the walkie-talkie that Dritan gave me yesterday. I heard Dritan's voice coming through the device.

"Hossan? Violeta? You there?" I picked up the walkie-talkie and pressed down on the button to talk.

"Yeah, we're here. We just woke up," I replied.

"Good. Anton and I are still getting everything ready. Get down here quick!" Dritan ordered.

"Roger that," I said in a joking tone. However, I still remained serious. "Come on, we've got to get to Dritan quickly if we want this thing to work," I said as I motioned for Violeta to get out of the bed. We got dressed, ready for the day, and headed out.

Violeta and I walked down the street and to our surprise, we saw something new. A lot of the people that we passed had guns or some kind of weapon in their hands. It was like a parallel universe where everyone was an action star in a movie. The Devilmen, along with a few other gangs, had been giving out guns like it was a charity. Of course not everyone had guns. There definitely weren't enough guns to arm all of the citizens of Roderic. To compensate, it looked like whoever didn't have a gun in their hands wielded bats, knives, and just about anything else they could use as a weapon. I saw a baker, walking out of his bakery clasping a rolling pin like a baton. Another, swinging a chain lock over his head like a medieval flail. People around smiled and waved at us, all because of the video I took. People walked up to me and thanked me for the video, for revealing the horrors of what the Perfects were doing and told me they felt safe knowing that I was standing up for the humans. I enjoyed the attention the people give me much more than the kind of attention the audiences gave me when I was a Perfect.

Violeta and I eventually made it to Dritan's headquarters. The foul smell lingering through the halls of the building greeted us. The men that guarded the building with their guns happily let the both of us through without question. One of them even fist-bumped me. As we headed downstairs into the basement, I heard the familiar sound of fingers tapping on keyboards. Along with the guys at the computers and the heroin makers, there were people rushing around the room hectically organizing loads of weapons.

At the end of the room I saw Anton, Dritan, and Bartek all talking to each other. I went quickly went over to see what was going on.

"Oh good, you're here," Anton said upon seeing me.

"Hey," I replied before immediately turning to Bartek.

"Bartek, what are you doing here?" I asked, confused.

"I'm here to help. These guys came and asked me to join and I said why not? You know?" Bartek said. He tried to sound casual about it but he seemed pretty excited about the whole thing.

"Do you even know what you're going to do?" I asked Bartek. Before he could answer, Anton interrupted him.

"Yeah, he does. We told him all about the plan. He's going to be part of the attack that's going to create the diversion," Anton explained. "At the same time, you and your girlfriend here, Dritan, and a couple other guys are going to get you to the government building."

Anton then turned to Dritan.

"Can you get the bags?" Anton asked.

"Yup," Dritan said as he went over to grab three large duffle bags. Dritan carried them back and dropped them in front of us.

"What's this?" I asked.

"The bombs," Dritan casually replied as he dropped the bombs right onto to the floor. I freaked out.

"Wait, *these* are the bombs!? Why would you just have them here!?" Dritan and Anton laughed as if it was all a joke.

"Don't worry. They're not even armed yet," Dritan said. "See?" he casually said as he unzipped one of the bags to reveal the bombs.

A collection of wires and strangely shaped metal devices filled the bag. Connecting all of the wires is a cellphone taped down to the bomb itself. Dritan then handed me a piece of paper with a cell phone number on it.

"Take it. It's the number to detonate the bomb. Put it into your phone," he commanded. I followed as ordered and added the number to my phone.

"There are four bombs in each bag so set them carefully and precisely. All of the bombs will go off as soon as you call that number, so just hold on to it for now. We'll tell you when you can blow it up," Anton explained.

"These are the targets here, here, and here." Anton circled on the map, writing our initials next to the circles.

Anton turned back to face Dritan. "This one's especially important because as long as you set the charges correctly, the buildings will sway and fall right into this power station," Anton said, making a circle on the map. "This power station feeds power to most of the buildings in the area. But some of the buildings, including the government building, have generators," Anton explained, pointing to the map.

"How do you know it's going to fall on the power station?" I asked.

"I know as much about engineering as you do with mopping up floors," Anton joked as he rolled up the map. "Oh wait, that reminds me..." Anton said before asking one of the computer guys to pull up a video. "Come look at this," Anton said, motioning for me.

I came over, Violeta following me. I saw some men attack a white van. They ran inside the van and were fighting with a couple of people. When they dragged out the men from the van, it became obvious that they were Perfects. They were kicked and pelted with stones until the video stopped.

"That video was taken last night during the curfew, which is great because it means people are starting to really get angry," Anton chimed in. "I've already sent out a message to the rest of the people in Roderic. They know what to do for the attack and they're definitely ready for it," Anton added, as he then took out his walkie-talkie and held it up to our faces.

"Stay in contact, let me know when you've all planted your bombs and then I'll tell you all what to do after you've done your jobs," Anton commanded. "Remember, we've only got one shot at this, people! Make sure you set the charges right up against the support columns. And be careful not to get caught. Like I said, we've only got one shot at this!"

With those last words, Dritan, Bartek, and I grabbed the bags and headed off. As I left the building, Violeta stopped me just outside the Devilmen headquarters.

"Be careful, okay?"

"I will. I'll be fine, don't worry." We hugged and Violeta gave me a peck.

"I'll be waiting for you," Violeta said to me. I nodded in confirmation just before I turned to leave.

The three of us boarded the same elevated train. We all sat down next to each other on the cold, plastic benches. It feels like we're moving at a snail's pace. With the weight of the duffel bag of bombs in my lap, I couldn't help thinking about how this would all turn out. I unzipped the bags just a little bit to see how the bombs looked. They seemed so complicated just by appearance that it would probably take me decades to figure out how to make one.

Just a few months ago, I was a normal janitor working in a mall that wasn't any different from all the other malls in Alpha. And now I was about to bomb a building in Alpha city and start a revolution against the Perfects. How did I get myself into this? Part of me felt like I wanted something like this. My dream was to find something different in my life. I'd hoped it would be winning the Lucky Day lottery, which turned out to be a big mistake for me. I realized that what I wanted to do was to stop the Perfects. With these bombs.

The train stopped at a station close to the building Dritan was going to bomb. As he stepped off of the train, Dritan turned around with a smile.

"Good luck!" He said it like this was all some kind of sick joke. It was just like him to do that.

Soon it was Bartek's stop. He tried to look cool and calm like Dritan but I could see the nervousness on his face.

"See you later, man."

"Yeah, see you later," I replied.

By the time I arrived at my stop, my body was shaking with anxiety. I pulled the strap of the duffle bag over my shoulder and ran off the train. I covered my face by pulling the neck hole of the shirt I was wearing over my nose. I needed to stay hidden as best as I could as long I was in Alpha. I quickly managed to find the building. It was so tall, when standing in front of it, it seemed like it was an elevator to the moon.

I entered the building and quickly maneuvered through the crowd of Perfects inside. The first thing that I felt was the fear of getting caught. Inside, giant security guards were posted against the walls of the lobby, each with giant rifles in their hands. If even one of the Perfects spotted me, I'd be done for. I sneaked over to the door to the stairwell and waited until the guards turned their heads away. The second they did so, I bolted straight through the door.

I quietly made my way downstairs into the underground parking lot. The only part of the parking lot that was illuminated was the pathway for the cars. I decided to move through the space between the wall and the cars. In this narrow space, it was dark enough for me to move around without being seen.

Making my way to each of the support structures, I saw that they were all wide in diameter. I suddenly felt a little speculative about whether these bombs could really knock down these enormous buildings. I took out one of the cell phone bombs from the duffel bag and carefully set it down next to one of the stone pillars. Even though Anton told me that the bombs would only go off with a call to the cell phone, I still felt like this thing was going to blow up in my hands. Moving from one corner of the lot to another, I carefully planted the bombs at each pillar. Sometimes I would have to crawl over the cars to stay unseen in the small space.

As I got close to the last pillar, I heard the sound of a car driving into the parking lot. It entered through a pathway surrounded by other cars. Its headlights were bright as the car moved closer to where I was. I panicked. I quickly jumped behind one of the other cars next to me to hide. Watching through the windows, I hid behind the parked car, waiting for my chance to move. The flash of the headlights passed by me and the car drove into an empty parking spot on the other side of the lot. The engine stopped, the lights turned off, and the driver door opened. A Perfect man stepped out of the car. He wore a fancy suit and held a brief case in his right hand. As he stepped into the middle of the parking lot under the lights, he looked down at his watch.

"Just leave already," I quietly mumbled to myself. As soon as the Perfect left I was free to do what I needed to do.

I quickly planted the last bomb and threw away the duffel bag. Covering my face with my shirt, I ran out of the building. I didn't want to take any chances with the possibility of the Perfects in the building finding me. I pulled out my walkie-talkie as I kept running through the crowds until I reached an alleyway. Nobody was around to hear or see me so I was safe. I turned on the walkie-talkie and called Anton.

"Anton! Anton can you hear me!?" I yelled, feeling absolutely terrified of getting caught. With the feeling of relief, I heard Anton's voice through the walkie-talkie.

"Loud and clear. What's up?" he replied.

"I finished planting the bombs. What about the others?" I asked.

"Good work, Hossan. The others are waiting for you back on the platform. They're all waiting for you."

"Thanks, I'll get there soon."

I quickly ran to the train station and rode the elevated train all the way back to Roderic. I sat on the plastic bench of the train with the feelings of nervousness and excitement. I started to take deep breaths in order to calm myself down. I opened up my cell phone to tell the time. It was 11:45 pm. By now, I thought, all of the people must be by the Big Gate, ready to attack.

As the train stopped at the station, I stood up from the bench. The doors flung open and I met with Dritan, Violeta, and two men that I'd never met before.

"Yo! How'd it go?" Dritan asked.

"Good," I replied.

I turned to look at the two men by Dritan. They were about the same height and build, and both wore dark hoodies and shorts with guns in their hands.

"Who're they?" I asked, pointing to the two.

"Oh, they're going to help protect us on our way to the government building," Dritan explained.

"Don't worry, we can handle whatever the Perfects throw at us!" One of them said as they both cocked their guns.

Violeta came to me and gave me a hug.

"Are you okay?" she asked as the train left the station, and the wind blew our hair to the side.

With the wind pulling her hair back, I could see Violeta's face clearly, and she looked clearly worried. But from the way she acted and sounded now, she must have been relieved to see me. I heard something in the distance as Violeta pushed away from me.

The sound was feint. I could only hear it when the train was gone. I stepped out to the edge of the platform to hear chanting from somewhere in the distance. I turned around.

"Do you hear that?" I asked. My voice muffled out the sound of the chanting. "You gotta be quiet to hear it, but it sounds like chanting."

"It is chanting," Dritan answered. "They're people chanting at the Big Gate. They're getting ready to attack," he explained.

I felt so proud in this moment. If only I could see what it looked like from down there.

"Hey check this out!" Dritan said as he walked up to me.

He showed me in his hand a strange, rectangular device with wires hanging out.

"What is it?"

"It's something Anton gave me," Dritan said as he handed me the device for me to study it. It was clunky with tangled wires. It felt like it was about to fall apart.

"It's a hacking device. He told me to use it to get through the security systems at the labs that you were talking about," Dritan explained.

"He built this? How long did it take?" I asked, impressed.

"I don't know. A day, maybe," Dritan casually answered.

I was still felt impressed over just how smart Anton was. I handed the device back to Dritan when I finished studying it.

I noticed the motorcycles behind Dritan and the others.

"These are the bikes we're going to use," Dritan explained as he walked over to one of the bikes.

"This one's mine," he said as he grabbed onto the handle bars. Both of Dritan's men walked over to two more parked motorcycles.

"These are ours," one of them explained as they pulled out the keys to their own bikes.

"Which one's mine?" I asked.

"Right over there," Dritan replied while pointing over to his right past the two others.

There, I saw it. It was the bright red, beautiful motorcycle that I'd always admired. The bike that I always looked at through Hendri's shop window but could never afford to buy. I slowly walked to it, in complete disbelief that this incredible piece of magnificent engineering was here for me.

"He... he just gave it to you?" I asked.

"Yup. He was happy to oblige for us revolutionaries," Dritan said. I gripped my hands onto the handles of the bike. It felt perfect in my hands.

"Hey!" Dritan called out to me. I turned around, and felt something small hit me in the chest. It dropped into my hands and I looked down at it. In my hands was the key to the bike. I smiled with extreme happiness at Dritan.

"Thank you!" I said, feeling so happy that I almost couldn't contain myself.

Dritan smiled back at me with his nice, normal smile.

"Come on, let's bring the bikes into the train tracks!" Dritan ordered.

We pushed the bikes down to the end of the platform and then down the service stairs onto the tracks. Carefully we lowered each bike down the stairs. I was especially careful with mine, not wanting to get a scratch on it.

"That's the last one!" Dritan called out, finally finished.

We all jumped into the tracks and hopped onto our motorcycles. I rested on the soft leather seat of the bike and Violeta sat behind me. I opened up my phone to look at the time. It was 11:58 pm.

"It's almost time," I said.

"Yeah..." Dritan replied as he looked up to the stars at night.

"Oh wait... I almost forgot," Dritan said as he opened out the kickstand of his bike and got off. Walking towards me and Violeta, he reached into his jacket pocket and presented two pistols.

"Here, you'll need these," he said as he pushed the guns towards us. I picked one of the pistols and shoved it into my jacket pocket. Violeta was hesitant to take the other one.

"You're not going to take one?" I asked to her.

"I've never used one before," she explained. I replied with a short laugh.

"Neither have I. There's a first time for everything, right?" I said.

Dritan continued holding out the gun to Violeta, not saying a word. Violeta slowly reached her hand out and picked up the pistol. Dritan nodded his head and spoke.

"Don't worry. Just aim and fire, easy," he said as he returned to his motorcycle.

I pulled out my walkie-talkie from my pocket and called Bartek.

"Bartek. How're things going on down there?" I asked, knowing that he was with the other rebels.

"Pretty good. Everyone's all riled up here by the Big Gate. I can see everyone's got their guns and stuff ready. The Perfects can see it, too. And I can tell the Perfects are starting to get a little nervous," Bartek said with a short laugh. I could hear the shouting and chants of everyone at the Big Gate in the background.

"Alright. You know what to do when the signal goes. Good luck," I said as I ended the call.

"Should be just about time," Dritan said. We all looked down at Alpha city from the train tracks, sitting on our bikes. The giant screens hanging from the sides of buildings showed the faces of Perfect celebrities at random. Each of them in their own pose, advertising something. I suddenly had a thought before everything started. I turned my head to meet Violeta's eyes.

"Hey, I need to tell you something."

"What is it?" Violeta replied.

"I just want you to know that I'm glad you're here with me. It's really been great knowing you," I said with a smile. Violeta hugged me from behind as she replied.

"Thanks."

"Oh yeah and one more thing I wanted to say."

"What is it?" I took in a deep breath, and spoke.

"When this is all over, let's get married." Violeta hesitated at first, but then she came up with her answer.

I quickly exclaimed, "Maybe we should go on a couple more dates first. It was just something on my mind."

"Okay", Violeta whispered while still embracing me as we waited for our time.

Suddenly, the siren signaling the curfew screamed across the city.

"This is it! Hossan, get your phone out!" Dritan ordered.

"Alright!" I said, as I pulled from my pocket the phone and the paper with the number for the cellphone bombs.

I turned on the phone and waited. As the sound of the siren kept screaming across the city, all lights of Roderic switched off automatically. Block by block, the city got darker while Alpha stayed bright. I dialed the number on the phone and held my thumb over the call button, waiting. The siren stopped and all of Roderic was dark, but not quiet. As soon as the siren stopped I could hear the chanting from the Big Gate getting louder and intensify. At that moment, I pressed down on the call button. Nothing happened.

"It didn't work?" Dritan asked, sounding disappointed.

"I don't know. Let me try agai-" Before I could finish speaking, the bombs went off.

I nearly fell off my bike from the force of the bombs. From where I was, I could clearly see all three buildings begin to lean over. As they fell, glass shattered and rained down onto the streets. The buildings all came down with such force and sound that it would make anyone standing within a half mile lose their hearing. The first two buildings collapsed on the tops of Perfects' heads and other buildings. The third building's bomb was detonated by Dritan.

He called out, "Hey! That one's mine!" He hollered excitedly as the third building crashed down on top of the power station, just as Anton had planned.

As soon as the building crashed down on the power station, every street lamp, most of the buildings, and all of the giant screens that once lit Alpha shut off.

The fighting started in the streets. I could hear gunfire from both the people and the Perfects.

"Alright that's our cue, let's go!" Dritan ordered as he and the other men pushed the keys into their bikes and started their engines. I followed, pushing in and turning the key. The purr of the engine made me feel only more excited.

"Let's go!" I yelled.

Violeta wrapped her arms tight around my hips. We all revved our engines and took off. Speeding down the train tracks, the darkness in Alpha began to appear closer to me. It made me feel so powerful that I could do something like this.

Speeding across the tracks on our bikes, we crossed the border into Alpha. I looked over and saw the people and the Perfects around the Big Gate. I witnessed gunfire. Live rounds being fired back and forth by the Perfects and the humans. In the background of the sounds of gunfire and chanting, I heard riot police yell out.

"Humans! Disperse immediately!" The rebels, of course, did the opposite.

When they heard the words, the humans pointed their guns at the Perfects. By the time the Perfects had their aim, they were already in a hail of bullets. The humans barely took the time to aim precisely. They mostly shot from the hip or from the shoulder, without caring about looking down the sights to aim. Only a few of the humans were shot while the Perfects were devastated in the first burst of fire. I witnessed men and women hurling Molotov cocktails at the Perfects. After laying waste to the dozen or so guards at the Big Gate, they ran into the streets of Alpha to continue shooting and burning. They came with such fury, most of them armed with more Molotov cocktails, guns, bats, hammers, and knives.

Out of nowhere, another siren rang out, but it sounded deeper than the siren used for the curfew. From the elevated tracks I saw soldiers clad in armor, with rifles and shields in their hands, flooding the streets of Alpha. At the same time, police drones were being mobilized like tanks to war. The soldiers were on one knee parallel to each other at one end of the street as the police drones continued down the street. The rebels moved in a giant, disorganized mass. All of them were waving their weapons in the air and angrily chanting.

"Down with the Perfects! Alpha's gonna burn!"

Their menacing chants echoed through city of Alpha. From the elevated tracks, I saw that there weren't any Perfect civilians around. They must've been told by police stay inside their homes. The drones stopped at the other side of the block as the police and soldiers.

The police drones opened up hatches at the end of their arms and six tubes emerged. Suddenly, the tubes shot out small cylinder-shaped canisters into the crowd of rebels. The canisters then quickly sprayed out large clouds of tear gas.

"Tear gas!" one of the rioters screamed.

Most of the people backed away from the gas. I saw others try to lob the canisters back at the police. Everyone was coughing as they tried to find their way through the mess as the gas consumed the entire block. The police drones and soldiers approached the tear gas cloud.

The last thing I saw from the clash was one of the police drones watching the tear gas cloud for any rebels when out of nowhere, a Molotov flew out of the tear gas and crashed into the police drone. Several rebels followed out of the cloud, firing their guns and continuing the chants. They ripped apart the first police drone with their bullets and moved onto the rest of the soldiers at the end of the road. Everyone was firing at each other. I couldn't hear myself think over the sound of gunfire from all sides.

When I rode on the motorcycle, it felt like the world was revolving around me with Violeta's arms tightly wrapped around my waist. As we approached a turn in the elevated train tracks, Dritan saw an opening. It was a three foot wide hole in the guard rail, definitely wide enough for the bikes to fit.

"Through there!" Dritan yelled, pointing to the opening in the guardrail.

Dritan and his men pulled in front and jumped off of the tracks and onto the streets. Their bikes disappeared in front of me when they jumped.

"Hold on!" I screamed to Violeta.

She squeezed onto my waist tighter as we approached the drop. I revved the engine hard and it suddenly felt like we were traveling at the speed of light. I felt weightless as the bike slipped off of the tracks. Violeta squeezed me so tight on the jump that I thought I would've split in two. I closed my eyes for a split second in a spark of fear. The bike hit the ground so hard I felt like I rode it off a skyscraper. I stopped the bike for a moment to get my composure back.

"You alright?" I asked Violeta. She was panting and trying to catch her breath.

"Yeah... yeah, I'm okay." Dritan and his men pulled up beside us on their motorcycles.

"Don't get too comfortable, we've still gotta get the people out of those labs you talked about. C'mon!" Dritan ordered.

We all rode our bikes as fast as we could down the street. Being the only sources of light in the streets, our headlights made us look like comets as we rode. I could hear gunfire and explosions of all kinds echoing through the city. The streets were clear of Perfects. But when I looked up, I saw the Perfects looking down on all of us from their apartments. I was sure the rebels would be around here soon. I felt the wind hit my face as we sped down the street; it was bliss. I had almost forgotten that I was in a revolution and that I was about to kill the Mayor of Alpha city. But the sounds of gunfire and explosions kept bringing me back to reality.

We finally pulled up in front of the lab. The lab didn't look too different from most other buildings in Alpha, at least not too different from the outside.

"C'mon! Let's go!" Dritan commanded.

His men pushed up front to lead us in with their guns. The two men blasted through the front door with their guns coming in first. They waved them around in all directions, their heads on a swivel, looking for any targets.

"No one's here," called out one of the men as all of the rest of us came into the building.

"Of course not. They're all in their homes trying to hope for the best," Dritan said as he strode into the room.

"Where do we go, Hossan?" Dritan asked. I pointed to the door which led into the stairwell.

"Through there."

I led the group up to the fourth floor. The sounds of our shoes clanging on the metal steps echoed through the stairwell. We reached the floor with the experimented humans and ran over to Jurica's cell.

"What the fuck is that thing!?" One of Dritan's men yelled out in disgust.

"It's one of the humans that the Perfects experimented on. His name is Jurica," I explained.

Jurica laid on the floor in the same position as I first found him, with his body like stone, and his head motionless on the floor. Jurica lifted his head up to see us all. His eyes fixed around everyone but his stares were mostly directed at me. With his eyes fixed right into mine, I once again felt as if he was looking straight into my soul.

Jurica slowly got to his feet, letting out deep breaths. He had more bruises now than before. The security guards must've beat him up with the batons again. Jurica walked up to the glass. He made no attempt to break down the glass barrier like last time. His eyes were dead set on mine. I motioned to Dritan who was standing next to me.

"Dritan... the keypad."

"I got it," Dritan replied.

He then walked up to the keypad to smash the cover with his gun. He ripped off the shattered cover, revealing the circuitry. Dritan connected the hacking device and turned it on. Automatically, the device began to hack the keypad. As we waited for the door to open, Jurica continued to stare at my eyes.

"Why is he staring at you?" one of the gangsters asked.

"I don't know," I simply answered, not wanting to talk about how Jurica mugged me. The glass barrier then slowly started to open like a garage door.

As soon as the barrier completely opened, Jurica slowly stepped out. He stood in front of us like a giant. My voice, along with my body, shook with intense fear.

"I told you I'd be back," I said with terror coursing through every fiber of my being, hoping that he wouldn't try to crush me.

Jurica then stretched out his massive hand to me. I thought he was about to shake my hand and I even reached out my own hand, but then he grabbed me up by my waist and crushed my arms in. I uttered an animal-like squeal and squirmed around as Jurica lifted me up off the ground.

Jurica lifted me right up to his face. I could smell the stench of his breath as it blew into my face. He could easily have crushed me to death with his gargantuan hands. Jurica looked around past me. His eyes darted to his right and he saw Dritan and his men standing parallel to each other. With guns drawn, their bodies didn't move an inch, their sights pointed at Jurica's head. He then looked to his left. He saw Violeta also holding up her gun. However she was trembling in fear, barely even holding onto the gun. Tears rolled down her cheeks as she kept moving her head side to side, like she was trying to say NO. However she couldn't say anything because her fear acted as a muzzle.

I tried to turn around to see what Jurica was looking at, but every time I squirmed, he tightened his grip on me even more. I felt like my ribs were about to break and my organs were about to be squished. Violeta had tears rolling down her cheeks, barely able to hold her gun steadily.

"Please... please don't," she said.

Jurica turned his head to face me again. He kept breathing in and out, his foul-smelling breath wafting into my face. Suddenly, Jurica let his grip loosen and softly placed me down on the floor. Back on my feet and free from Jurica's grip, Violeta took a deep breath of relief as she put away her gun.

Jurica walked slowly over down the hall towards the lab, passing Dritan and his men, their guns still on Jurica. He stopped in the middle of the hallway and faced the wall opposite from the glass barriers. Jurica took one more look at Violeta, his eyes studying her face and soul.

Jurica then got into a stance with his head forward, knees bent, and his giant fists tightly clenched. He quickly moved towards the concrete wall in front of him with his two fists together. With one swift motion of brute force, Jurica smashed his fists against the wall. Immediately, a giant crack appeared on the wall. The impact caused an earth-shattering surge of force that rocked through the ground. He hit the wall again, and again we all felt the same wave of power under our feet. The wall started to break apart. Jurica could see how the outside world looked through the small holes in the wall he created. He smashed his fists into the wall and began to feel the cool night air passing over his body. We all felt it pass over us.

He kicked out the last pieces and punctured a massive hole in the once solid concrete wall. Jurica then pushed himself through the wall and jumped out. None of us saw him land. All we heard was a loud thud. We all ran over to the hole to see Jurica running down the street.

"Where do you think he's going?" I asked.

"I don't know. But he's definitely not coming back here," Dritan replied.

I turned my head to the large metal door at the end of the hallway.

"This way!" I yelled as I quickly made my way to the room where they stored countless others like Jurica.

Everyone else followed. I opened the door and the entire hallway behind me was filled with light from the room. Nothing about this room had changed. Giant, brightly lit, and full of experimented humans that look exactly like Jurica. Except this time, no guards were around to catch us. They must have been too busy dealing with the attack.

"So this is where they keep all of the other ones," one of Dritan's men said as the other man's jaw dropped in horror. I spotted a control panel near the other cages.

"Over here," I said while walking over to the control panel.

I spotted a bright red button in the middle.

"Look. This one says emergency release," I announced.

The moment he heard me say the word, Dritan yelled out, "Let's hit it!" And he smashed his fist down on the button.

Instantaneously, all of the glass cell blocks opened up. I thought they'd all jump out immediately now that they were free. At first, the creatures were hesitant, but then they looked around and saw that there weren't any guards. They saw that this wasn't some sort of trick, it was really happening. They all quickly jumped out. They landed on the floor with such force that I thought the whole world would've collapsed on itself. Every one of the creatures piled on top of each other, shoving to get through to the exit. We knew where they were headed, and as long as we stood in their way, we'd be crushed.

"Move! Go now!" Dritan screamed. We all ran out of the room as the creatures followed us.

We all ran for the staircase door. Dritan and his men flung it open and ran through. Violeta and I followed them. Jumping out of the way of the creatures and into the stairwell at the last second, I landed on top of Violeta. I didn't look behind me. I could only hear the creatures running past us and crashing around in the hallway. Hearing the creatures run past us like this was like listening to a freight train from hell pass us.

Once all of the noise stopped, I stood and helped Violeta up. We walked into the hallway and it looked as if a tornado had just ripped through. All of the lights were smashed and cracks covered the walls. A pile of twisted metal was all that was left of the door to where the creatures had been stored.

I felt a strong breeze coming from down the hall. I followed the wind to the hole that Jurica had just made. Only now, the hole was much larger. It had to be at least twenty feet wide.

"Damn..," one of Dritan's men said in awe.

We watched as the creatures frantically ran in all directions down the streets. I could hear the sound of gunfire in the background, and once again, I could feel the cold night air on me.

"Come on, let's get outta here!" I commanded.

Everyone followed me outside to the bikes. We knew exactly where to go… the Alpha city government building.

The engine of my motorcycle roared under me with Violeta's arms around my waist. Dritan and his men followed us as we drove lightning-fast through Alpha. With heavy intent in our minds, we barreled down the street at a hundred miles per hour. We spotted a tall, brightly lit building, still with no sign of anyone outside. We all pulled up to the curb in front of the government building.

"Alright, ready?" I asked, trying to motivate everyone.

"Yeah!" Everyone cheered.

"Alright, let's go!" I said.

Just as we got off of the motorcycles, we heard the roaring sound of helicopter blades flapping over us like a dragon. We all looked up and saw cannons and missiles attached to the attack helicopter. It was a frightening sight to see.

It flew past us and started to fire its weapons, creating giant fiery explosions on the street ahead of us. A group of humans and the creatures ran down the street. We watched as the humans were gunned down and run over by armored cars at an intersection at the end of the street.

"Dammit, we gotta help them!" Dritan said as he turned around to his men.

"Go! Go help 'em out!" Dritan ordered, waving his gun in the direction of the rebels in need of help. Dritan's men immediately sped off on their motorcycles to help the other rebels.

"I'll go, too!" Violeta said. I immediately froze upon hearing those words from Violeta. I think Dritan had the same feeling. I quickly turned to face her. I knew in my head, there was no way I was letting her go into that carnage.

"Absolutely not! I'm not letting you go! You can't! NO WAY!" I yelled in her face to suppress her.

At first, her face expressed sadness and fear. But soon, her eyebrows scrunched in, she made tight fists and spoke with a voice like a cannon.

"I'm going to help, and there's nothing you can do to stop me! This is my moment!" she said with unwavering resolve.

My mouth gaped open, not a single word coming out. I felt like an idiot just standing there with nothing to say at all. With mirror-like eyes, Violeta stared me down, continuing to show unrelenting courage. The terrifying sounds of gunfire and explosions continued on in the background. I kept standing there, completely disregarding the havoc around us.

"Okay..," I said softly, then I brought Violeta as close as possible to me for a hug.

"Just come back safe, please." I grasped her tightly in my arms. "Please..."

She was everything to me. I wouldn't ever let anything to happen to her, but at same time, I wanted her to be brave and do her own things. She then wrapped her arms around me.

"Thank you."

She sat on my motorcycle and revved the engine, making it purr. She picked up her helmet and held it over her head. Violeta was about to squeeze the helmet onto her head but I stopped her for a moment. I leaned in to her lips to give her one more, and possibly, my final kiss. Our lips parted.

"You know what to do. Come back safe," I said, letting her go.

"You, too," Violeta replied. I nodded and then turned to Dritan.

"Good luck," he said, and for the first time, Dritan sounded genuinely serious. The two of them then sped off on their motorcycles to help the other rebels.

Turning my attention to the government building, I pulled out the pistol that Dritan had given me and pulled the hammer back. The sound of the click created by the hammer echoed through my head. I slowly took a deep breath to calm my beating heart. I needed to calm myself down to make my aim steady. I started to think about Violeta and the moments we shared. The memories of us together helped me settle down enough to continue with what I had to do. I strode to the front doors with confidence and determination. Moving inside with the pistol extended out, I saw neither a single human nor any Perfects. I moved into the nearest elevator and pushed the button for the top floor.

The elevator started to climb up the massive building. Halfway up inside the elevator, the glass walls let me take in the view of all of Alpha. All of the lights were still out. The fires lit the night sky and the streets in a deep hues of orange and red. Burning cars, burning buildings and gunfire were the things that I saw the most. I looked down to see the rebels in the streets. They were gunning down as many Perfects as they could see. Not just the soldiers, but the civilians too. The civilians must've thought it'd be better to make a break for it instead of waiting to have their doors broken down by the rebels. I guess that decision didn't prove as ingenious as they might've thought.

I looked ahead to see the tall buildings. The ones that were burning stood out the most to me. But then I saw the buildings that weren't burning. The creatures from the labs were climbing up the buildings and towers. They smashed their hands into the walls to scale the building. I saw creatures smash their hands through the windows of the buildings as they climbed, and then they'd pull out a fistful of Perfects. Sometimes just one, and sometimes three of them at once. The creatures tossed them away to smash against the pavement, and then they'd just keep climbing. I stared at the view for as long as I could. It was truly a horrifying sight, but it was just what I wanted, what needed to happen.

I heard a ding behind me. The elevator doors opened and I stepped out into a long, white-walled, brightly-lit hallway lined by a long red carpet. A single, giant gold door stood at the end of the hallway. I had my pistol to my side with the safety off so that I was ready to shoot. I slowly opened the door. Peering into the room, I saw the Mayor with his back to me, standing behind his desk, looking out the window at the chaos below.

"You've made quite a mess in my city today, Hossan." He then turned around as he spoke. "I hope you don't plan on getting away with this."

He started to walk to his desk. I saw that he was reaching for something in a drawer of his desk. I quickly aimed my gun at the Mayor.

"Don't move! Put your hands up!" I ordered, my pistol shaking in my hands.

I could feel drops of sweat rolling down my back from the anxiety that was crushing me. The Mayor stopped reaching and stepped back from his desk with his hands slightly up.

"So what are you going to do now, Hossan?" he said casually, as if there wasn't a gun pointed at him. "What are you going to do? Kill me?" the Mayor asked in a cynical tone, challenging me, with his hands still up. Trying to maintain my composure as well as a steady aim, I answered.

"No, I'm not. I'm taking you to Roderic so you can finally face justice."

"I'm sorry to tell you this, Hossan, but that's not going happen, not by a long shot. No matter what you do, you're screwed."

He kept his hands to his sides as he spoke.

"You see, Hossan, Jack Miller was an absolute gold mine just like the rest of the humans who were turned into Perfects. We had it all figured out, too. We had Jack Miller figurines, video games, tons of ads, and even a limited edition collectible sneaker line. We were even going to put out a feature film for everyone to see! But you just had to go and ruin it all," He explained. "And for what!?" The *May*or yelled, demanding an answer.

"Do you have any idea how many lives you've ruined!? Don't you have enough money!?" I yelled.

He laughed as he put his hands into his pockets. "Nope. And you know what? We've got our own people problem too!" he shouted, attempting to convince me. "The population of Perfects is increasing. And since the Perfects rely on Formula-H for survival, we need more. That's where the humans come in! For a while now, we've been kidnapping humans because they didn't want to try to win the lottery anymore. It's all a way to speed up the process, you know?" The Mayor let out a short little laugh before speaking again. "By the way, the "H" in Formula H, it stands for human."

My blood was at its boiling point after hearing his words. I stormed over to the Mayor and pushed the barrel of my pistol against his forehead. He didn't even flinch, nor did he ask for mercy. He only stared down the barrel of my pistol and then back down to me. I yelled at him angrily, trying my damnedest to intimidate him.

"I'm gonna kill you now, you son of a bitch! I'm going to blow your goddam brains out!"

"Then do it already you moron! If you're gonna point a gun at me ya gotta have the balls to shoot!" He yelled, unafraid of me. "You're not going to do anything to hurt me. I'll still be in power, and you'll be the one who'll die," He said, sounding satisfied with himself.

"Just shut up! Now, I'm going to give you to the count of three to come with me to Roderic, or else I'm going to shoot!" I threatened.

"More than enough time," the Mayor laughed.

We stared coldly into each other's eyes as I pushed the barrel of my pistol up to his forehead.

"One..." I said, keeping my finger on the trigger.

"Two..." My hands were shaking so much that I thought I was going to drop my gun.

Suddenly the door to the Mayor's office burst open. It was so startling that it caused my skin to tingle. I turned my head, and behind me stood one of the Mayor's security agents, his pistol aimed at my back. I froze in fear.

"Hey, Hossan," the agent said nonchalantly.

I instantly recognized that voice. I was already afraid but hearing that voice shook me to my core.

"Remember me?" he asked. I hesitated. I couldn't form words. I kept the gun pointed at the Mayor but my eyes were locked on Tony.

Out of nowhere, I felt my gun move by itself. I turned and realized that the Mayor pushed it out of the way to lay a direct punch to my face. I fell hard to the ground and dropped my pistol. I quickly reached out for my gun but before I could grab it, the Mayor slammed his foot onto my hand. I let out a short scream of pain as the Mayor grinded my carpals under his shoe.

"You lost this one, Hossan," the Mayor chuckled as he knelt down to grab my gun. "We owned you then, and we still own you now," the Mayor scoffed as he examined my gun and aimed it down on my forehead.

This is the end, I thought. I won't ever be able to see Violeta or anyone ever again. I tightly closed my eyes, bracing for death.

"You know, I can't really get what you said out of my head... about justice," he said.

I looked up to see the Mayor still had the pistol aimed at me. I tilted my head up and saw Tony watching as the Mayor continued to talk.

"Justice. I can't think of a word more adored by the people. What justice, Hossan? What kind of justice does tearing up my city do?" he asked, shrugging his shoulders. "And just to make my words crystal clear, I wanna emphasize! You come to my city, you kill as many people as possible and then you burn it all to the ground! What kind of justice is that!?" the Mayor screamed. Ignoring everything he had to say, I kept my mind closed like a vice. Impossible for him to get into my head.

"The justice you're talking about sounds pretty rotten to me," the mayor finished as he pressed the barrel of the gun against my forehead. "Goodbye."

Suddenly, a powerful rumbling shook the room, coming from behind the door and down the hallway. The Mayor, Tony and I all turned to face the source of the sound. The rumbling quickly became louder and soon turned into a full-on stampede. The door burst open and a crowd of people stormed in.

"What the hell!?" Tony yelled.

Tony then shot into the crowd of humans. Out of nowhere, Violeta emerged from the crowd with fierce gracefulness. She quickly pistol-whipped Tony in the face, breaking off the bottom half of his smile mask.

His mouth and nose were exposed. He held his hand to his mask in pain. As he tried to raise his pistol up to the humans, they surrounded him, stomping him mercilessly. I watched as Tony oozed blackish fluid from his mouth and nose as the humans crushed their boots into his body.

I noticed that the Mayor was trying to aim his pistol at the crowd of people but, more specifically, at Violeta. I immediately sprang into action and tackled the Mayor to the ground, making him drop his pistol. He tried to reach out for the gun, but I grabbed the back of his shirt collar and pulled him up. I then slammed his body against the large glass windows. I punched him in the jaw and kicked him in the gut until he felt too groggy to fight back. He was obviously disoriented and could barely stand up straight. I quickly squared up and landed one final punch right into his jaw. His head violently curled back. He collapsed to the ground as he coughed and groaned in pain. I hopped over the Mayor's battered body and quickly grabbed my pistol.

Suddenly the fighting stopped. Everyone was panting from the fighting, myself included. Tony's body was in pieces after what the people did to him. The humans all gathered around behind me. Violeta stood next to me with her pistol in her hand. We all watched the Mayor struggle to get balance.

"Well Mayor, do you have any last words?" I said, confidently.

The Mayor only responded with laughing. Not a single word, just laughing, as if it was all a big joke. I couldn't think of a reason why he'd think we were joking around. As he kept laughing, I aimed my pistol to the Mayor's head. Violeta and all of the other humans followed. Everyone raised their pistols, shotguns, and rifles to line up parallel with each other, all aiming for the Mayor. I didn't take my eyes off him, and neither did anyone else.

I fired the first shot. Immediately, everyone else fired off their weapons. I could feel all of the bullets flying past me from behind. Some of the bullets ripped through him like it was nothing, shattering the glass windows behind him.

Whatever was left of the Mayor's body was forced out of the shattered windows by the bullets that pierced his body. Once he fell through, the shooting stopped. I walked over to the window and looked down to see his body fall a thousand stories, exploding into chunks of flesh as he smashed into the curb.

It was nearly silent in the room. The only sound was from people shuffling their feet through the bullet casings. The sounds of continued gunfire and explosions continued on from all across the city. I heard someone behind me in the crowd speak up.

"What do we do now?"

At that instant, I had an idea.

"I know what we could do," I said as I grabbed Violeta's hand.

The rebels made a hole for Violeta and me to walk through. We made our way to the elevator and everyone followed. Making our way outside, I hopped on my motorcycle. As I started the engine and Violeta sat on the back seat, she asked, "Where are we going?"

"You'll see," I replied as I revved the engine.

As we sped off, the crowd of rebels that followed us out clapped and cheered. The engine of my motorcycle roared across the city, signaling our victory. Cheers from our fellow humans surrounded us as we rode past them all. Violeta's arms were wrapped around me as I continued to ride down the road. With the wind blowing around us, we passed the burning wrecks of police cars and drones, all burning in a brilliant orange. Riding through the Big Gate and into Roderic, the cheers only grew louder.

"Do you want to tell me where we're going now?" Violeta asked.

"Don't worry, you'll see," I replied.

We rode through Roderic, eventually coming to a screeching stop. When everyone saw my face, they cheered just like the rest. Violeta and I got off the bike and I led her into the park. People followed as I walked with Violeta, holding hands with her. We eventually made it to the biggest hill in the park. Violeta and I climbed up the hill and a crowd of people followed us.

We got a clear view of Alpha city from the top of the hill. It burned bright as the sun, and even though the moonlight was blocked out with thick, black smoke, the city lights of Roderic made it clearer. Strangely, I never knew Roderic's lights were so bright at night. They must've always been outshined by Alpha's lights, preventing anyone from seeing how beautiful Roderic looked at night.

With hundreds of people behind us, Violeta and I watched Alpha burn to the ground. Some faint shooting could still be heard from Alpha.

Watching Alpha city burn, I turned my eyes to Violeta, maybe go in for a kiss. Watching her beautiful eyes brighten at seeing the view, I knew she didn't want to miss a second of witnessing this moment. Instead of interrupting view with a kiss, I simply reached out and held her hand.

Hossan laid completely motionless, like a stone. His skin was wrinkled and his body was paper thin, barely able to move. Nutrients were being pumped into him through thin tubes. A heart rate monitor hooked up to Hossan beeped at a steady pace, along with the steady pace of the harvesting machine pumping out Hossan's fluids. The automatic doors opened and two men walked into the room. It was Mayor Rollins and one of the Perfect scientists working in the labs.

"What's its condition?" the Mayor asked.

"Stable. We're keeping a close eye on it. We've put it in an unconscious state where we've generated a dream for this human to experience so that he wouldn't suddenly wake up again. We're now checking on the mental condition of every human we have here," the Perfect scientist explained to the Mayor as they walked up to Hossan's container.

The pace of the beeping from Hossan's heart rate monitor suddenly began to slow.

"Since the day of Hossan's escape, we began conducting routine sweeps of every human in this, and every other lab in Alpha. So far, there's nothing out of the ordinary to report," the scientist explained.

"Good. We can't possibly let something like this happen to us again," the Mayor replied sternly as he stared at Hossan's unconscious face. "If even one person on the outside knew about what we were doing here, it'd be the end for all of us."

The Mayor then turned to the Perfect scientist to ask him.

"What did you make as the dream for the human?"

"When we captured him back, we assessed his mental condition to determine exactly what went wrong. From there, we were able to find out what was in his head that made him escape. We created a dream for him based on his desires so that he wouldn't feel like waking up. A nice dream, you know? What I mean is, you're less likely to wake up from a good dream than a nightmare." He explained. "Basically, he wanted to kill you, and to be with some human girl."

The Mayor scoffed. "Whatever. We're extremely lucky that those police drones managed to corner and capture Hossan in that alley. Again, if anyone knew what we were doing, it'd be the end of us all." The scientist nodded in agreement. "Still, I almost feel sorry for them," the Mayor said. The Perfect scientist faced the Mayor in confusion at his statement.

"Almost," the Mayor added.

At that moment, the steady pace of the beeping from Hossan's heart monitor suddenly turned into one continuous beep. After a short pause, the Mayor clapped his hands together to break the silence.

"Okay let's get outta here. I never like being around these things for too long," he said as he motioned to the door.

"Tell me about it," the scientist groaned as he and the Mayor walked out of the room.

At the same time, the numbers of the Lucky Day lottery were announced. A poor, sickly old man was holding onto a crumbled up lottery ticket in his dirty hands. From an old radio, the man listened to the announcer read the winning numbers. The poor man read the numbers on his ticket at the same time that they were announced. It was an exact match. The man's eyes widened, and he hollered and cheered in great pride and happiness at the winning numbers on his ticket.

After Hossan left, Violeta continued her normal daily routine of eat, sleep, and work. She managed to take Hossan's old job as a janitor in the shopping mall where he used to work. By working two jobs, one at the supermarket and one as a janitor, Violeta was able to buy the things she needed and also a small amount of heroin for every once in a while. One day, as she was mopping the floors in mall, all the Perfects walking past without even glancing down to her, she suddenly heard a voice call out for her from out of nowhere.

"You are amazing!" Violeta turned around to see Jack Miller on a screen advertising a clothing line.

"I can see it in your eyes!" Jack Miller confidently exclaimed. Violeta stopped mopping for second to watch the ad as it finished. "Do you dare reach up to the stars and challenge the world?"

END

CPSIA information can be obtained at www.ICGtesting.com
Printed in the USA
BVOW08s0905150216

436756BV00001B/37/P